BECOMING BROOKE

QUINN VALLEY RANCH BOOK 6

KAY P. DAWSON

PROLOGUE

"What in heaven's name were you thinking, climbing up a ladder to hang Christmas lights at your age? Honestly, Maude, sometimes you don't have the sense of an old goat." Gertrude Quinn shook her head and clucked her tongue as she walked over beside the hospital bed of her friend.

"Well, how was I supposed to know I was going to fall? I wanted my Christmas lights up, and in case you haven't noticed, there aren't any young men hanging around my house to do it for me, so I did it myself. And I'd have been fine too, if not for that gust of wind that caught me off guard. Once I lost my balance, I went down harder than a sack of rocks."

The other ladies who were always together made their way around the bed. "Now, Maude, Gertie has plenty of grandsons who would have helped you if you'd asked, and I could have even told Ciran to help you. Now that the weather is colder, he's not as busy in the taco truck, so he'd have gladly agreed. You just won't accept that you're older now and shouldn't be doing silly things like climbing a ladder." Nellie pulled her jacket off as she scolded Maude.

Maude rolled her eyes and huffed loudly. "Betty...Ruby...do either of you have anything to add? Because right now, I'm on enough painkillers to not give a wit what anyone has to say, so you may as well get it all out. Just because *you're* all old, doesn't mean *I* am. I seem to remember that I'm the youngest out of the bunch of you."

"Well, you may be the youngest, but you're certainly not the smartest." They all laughed at Ruby's joke. Well, everyone except Maude.

"And now what will you do? You've got yourself a broken hip and a broken wrist. How are you going to take care of yourself?"

Maude didn't have any children of her own. Her husband had passed away well over ten years ago, leaving her alone. But until now, she'd never needed anyone to help her.

"I spoke to my niece in Pennsylvania. She said she would have come out to help but she's got a lot going on. So she's asked my great-nephew, Jared, if he could come out to stay here for a while. I already spoke to him this morning and tried to tell him he didn't have to come, but he told me in no uncertain terms he was already on his way. He said he could use a vacation." Maude smiled and shook her head. "He always has been a stubborn boy and I admit to having a bit of a sweet spot for him."

The women chatted for a while, having their usual Wednesday morning coffee right there in the hospital room instead of at Gertie's like they normally did. The coffee wasn't as good, but they weren't the type to complain.

"Oh, Gertie. I forgot to mention that Brooke came in to see me yesterday after I got out of my surgery. She was here checking on a few of her other patients from Quinn Valley who were admitted to the hospital, so she stopped to make sure they were taking good care of me. They'll be releasing me back into her care once I get home and she's assured me she will come around to the house to check on my progress instead of making me go into her office. She's a sweet girl, that granddaughter of yours."

"Yes, she is. But I worry that with her work, she'll never find time to settle down with anyone. I know her sister has been making her go on some dates—

using some site on the Internet, if you can imagine! But Brooke's heart has never really been in it. It's hard for her to trust after what that young man did to her two years ago." The other women all nodded sadly, knowing exactly what Gertrude was referring to. There were no secrets between the friends.

Suddenly, Gertie gasped and grabbed onto Maude's arm. "That nephew of yours, Jared. How old did you say he is? Is he married?"

Maude's mouth opened wide, then quickly turned into a smile as she got caught up in the excitement. "He's not married. And he's in his early thirties, so just about the perfect age for what you're thinking!"

"Does he have a good job? I don't want my Brooke to end up with some slacker who will rely on her money just because she's a doctor."

Maude scowled slightly at Gertrude. "My nephew is a good man, and he'd make anyone a fine husband. He's an author, you know. So he won't need money from anyone. And I happen to know he's a perfect gentleman." She lifted her nose a bit higher as she tucked the blankets around herself. "He would certainly be better than any of those men she could be dating from some website on that *Internet* thing."

"Oh, this is so exciting." Betty clapped her hands together sharply as the women all started to discuss what could happen.

"Of course, with Jared staying with you, and Brooke having to come by your house often to check up on you, it will be perfect. We might just have to move our coffee date over to your house next week to make sure these two will be suited for each other and that she doesn't suspect anything." Gertrude smiled innocently at her friends. "After all, you do know how I hate to meddle in my grandchildren's affairs."

CHAPTER ONE

Please, if it's not too much to ask, just burn this restaurant down around me. I promise I'll make sure everyone survives...

Brooke gave her head a quick shake. *No!* What was she thinking! She shouldn't be wishing Quinn's would burn down just for her sake. Her poor cousins who owned the popular Quinn Valley restaurant didn't deserve to be punished like she was being at the moment. She just wished she knew what she'd ever done to be forced to endure this torture.

"And every doctor I've seen tells me it's just a mole, but I'm not convinced. If nothing else, it at least has to be a wart. I'd show you right now, but as I mentioned, it's in a place that I can't really show in public." The man across the table grinned at her and wiggled his eyebrows up and down. "But, maybe later I can show you."

This couldn't seriously be happening. Surely, she was having a nightmare. All she could think right now was how much she was going to strangle her sister Robyn when she saw her again. It had been her idea to try these dating websites, and no matter how good any of the profiles claimed to be, the people she ended up meeting didn't match those descriptions at all. This wasn't the first time one of her dates had mentioned the possibility of her checking out their wart.

And the worst part was, she'd already arranged for another one tomorrow afternoon outside Ciran's taco truck. The only thing that soothed her was knowing there was no way it could ever be worse than the date she was sitting through right now. And maybe the warm weather would turn bad and a sudden snowstorm would blow in, saving her from more torture.

After the date tomorrow, she was done. *No more.* She didn't care if she did die a crazy old cat lady like her siblings kept insinuating was going to happen. Of course, she knew they were really only trying to get her back out there after the heartbreak she'd been through. They were concerned about her and didn't want to see her holing up in her apartment and using her job as an excuse not to try again.

"I really hate to bother you, Brooke, but Grams just called and wondered if you could run out and check on her? She says she's not feeling well." Her cousin Ivy was waiting the tables tonight and was looking at her with her eyes wide and jaw clenched as she kept her back turned slightly to her date. She gave a quick tilt of her head toward the back of the bar where her other cousins, Maggie and Ryder, stood grinning. "Ryder says you can use his car parked out back."

Even if she hadn't seen their expressions, Brooke wouldn't have believed Ivy. Her grandma Gertie was never sick. Apparently, she didn't have time for that kind of nonsense.

So Brooke wasn't really worried. She'd told Ryder earlier that if it looked like she needed help, he'd better step in to save her. It had taken him long enough, but at least he'd finally sent her a lifeline.

"Oh, I'm so sorry, Lance. But I really will need to go." She pulled her purse out, thinking if she at least offered to pay it might show she was slightly disappointed the date had to end. She pulled out some bills, waiting for him to decline the offer, but he gladly took the money and nodded.

"This should cover your share."

Brooke almost laughed out loud at the expression on Ivy's face. The poor girl stood with her jaw open, unable to move as her eyes locked on the man at the table.

"It was nice to meet you, Lance. Thank you for the...um, for the *interesting* evening." Brooke struggled to find the words to describe what she'd been through without telling him she'd have rather sat and had someone stab forks in her eyes for the past hour.

She really didn't want to be mean.

"So, can I call you again?" Lance stood up as she pushed her own chair back and flung her purse over her shoulder. *Couldn't he see her urgency?* She had a sick grandmother to check on!

Thankfully, Ryder must have noticed her panic and walked over with his keys in his hand. "You better hurry. She sounded awful when she called."

"I'm sorry, I really do need to go." She grabbed the keys from Ryder, ignoring the smirk she could see him trying to hide. But as soon as her fingers wrapped around the cold keys, her heart dropped when she looked at the restaurant door.

Her "sick" grandmother had just walked in the door, laughing with her friends.

Why couldn't Grandma Gertie be like other

grandmas and stay at home on a Friday night doing something useful, like knitting?

Maggie must have seen her come through the door at the same time they had, so she rushed over and whispered in her grandma's ear, before grabbing her arm and practically dragging the woman into the kitchen. Luckily, Brooke's date wouldn't know who her grandma was, so even if he had noticed the poor woman being hauled away, he wouldn't know that's who she was.

All Brooke could think was that there had to be some hidden cameras somewhere. Surely this was all some big prank.

Ryder took her arm and pulled her away, leaving Lance to finish up the chocolate cake on his own. All she could do was hope he would hurry up and leave, and that her grandma's friends hadn't noticed she'd been with him. Knowing those women, they'd all go over and introduce themselves to see who he was and ask whether or not Brooke was dating him.

Of course, that would be right before they announced that he should meet her grandma who was fit as a fiddle, standing in the kitchen behind them.

"It took you long enough. I'm sure I sent enough signals that even Batman is likely on his way. Next time I'll be sure to bring a large sign to hold up saying I could use some help, to make it easier for you."

Ryder just laughed as he pushed the door to the kitchen open. On the other side stood her poor grandma with a look of complete shock and confusion on her face.

"Would someone mind explaining to me what is going on? I don't believe for one second that Bethany needed my help figuring out how to make some new recipe." Ryder's fiancé was the chef at the restaurant, and everyone knew there wasn't anything she couldn't cook. She was standing beside the stainless-steel counter holding a large spatula in her hand and looking just as confused as Grandma Gertie.

"Grandma, it's my fault. You just need to stay back here for a couple of minutes until my date leaves."

"What are you talking about, Brooke? Are you afraid I'm going to embarrass you in front of your date?" Gertie's eyes pulled together, and Brooke was afraid she was about to get a scolding.

"No! It's not that at all." Although Brooke didn't want to mention that she had no doubt in her mind her grandma *would've* been over there in a heartbeat if she'd noticed she was on a date. "I had to pretend that you weren't feeling well, and you needed me to come out and take a look at you. The man I was on a date with wasn't exactly a good match."

Her grandma came over closer and crossed her arms in front of her chest. "Well, now, Brooke, why would you agree to go out on a date with a man who wasn't a good match?"

She had to fight not to roll her eyes in frustration. "Because I hadn't met him until tonight, Grams. And his profile had neglected to mention that he was a terrible bore and was most likely just looking for free medical advice about a wart he has on his privates."

Brooke enjoyed the shocked look on her grandma's face. "Well, that's awful. Let me see what this man looks like." Gertie was already headed to the doorway, pushing it open a crack to peek out into the restaurant.

"Grams, be careful! If he sees some gray-haired woman spying on him from the back, he might start to suspect something."

Her grandma just slapped at her hand as she tried to pull her away from the door. "Don't be ridiculous, Brooke. He isn't going to see me. Now, is that your young man there?" She moved aside slightly to let Brooke see out.

Lance was just standing up, talking to Ivy who was giving him his receipt from the machine.

"He's not *my* young man, Grams. And yes, that's him."

They watched him walk to the door and Brooke had to admit he was a good-looking man. Maybe that's what had attracted her to him when she'd been scrolling through the profiles. Was she really that shallow? Had she not noticed any signs that he wouldn't be a good match for her because she'd been so drawn to the chiseled jaw and bright blue eyes?

When he was finally out of the restaurant, Brooke breathed a loud sigh of relief and leaned back against the wall.

"If any of you ever have to wonder why I don't date, now you know."

Her grandma put her hand on her arm. "You just haven't found the right one yet, dear. But don't you worry. I have a good feeling that will happen sooner than you think."

Before Brooke could question her, Grandma Gertie walked out the door and back into the restaurant. Slowly, her eyes moved to Ryder and Maggie. "What does she mean by that?"

A sinking feeling full of dread filled her stomach.

Her grandma was up to something.

CHAPTER TWO

"I promise you, you have never had a taco as good as the ones Nellie's grandson makes. I never even realized how much I could love a taco until he showed up in town."

Jared smiled at his aunt as he pulled his jacket up around his shoulders. It was already the first of December, so there was a chill in the air, even if the weather was unseasonably warm today. Maude was lucky it wasn't below freezing, or he would never have agreed to stand outside at some taco truck to get her something she was craving.

When he walked outside, the warmth of the sun hit his cheeks and he was shocked to realize just how nice the day actually was. It wouldn't be a hardship to be out in some fresh air, waiting for his tacos.

Maude had mentioned there was a sit-down eating area used during the warmer months, so he could always wait at one of the tables. How busy could a taco truck really be anyway?

He hummed along to the song on the radio as he let his eyes move around to take in the sights of Quinn Valley. He'd been here for a couple of days now, but he really hadn't had much chance to look around to see what had changed. When he'd been a young boy, he used to come and spend a week or two each summer with his aunt, enjoying time away from the city where he'd grown up. It was always so much more peaceful and laid-back in the small town, and whenever he'd go home, he would spend the next few months wishing he could go back.

He'd always told himself that when he grew up, he was going to move somewhere as quiet and serene as Quinn Valley, but for some reason over the years, he'd forgotten how much nicer it was to be in a little town like this. The air seemed cleaner, the people friendlier, and the days slower and more relaxed.

Maybe he was going to have to consider it again. It wasn't like he couldn't live wherever he wanted with his job.

He smiled as he recognized the pale purple Victorian house, with the scalloped gingerbread trim that stood on one end of Main Street. A large sign announced the home of *Earth Mother,* the store his aunt had told him about. She'd been hinting that perhaps he might be able to go there and find some crystals or stones, or some other kind of new-age material that could help speed up her healing time.

He'd said he would wait until she was able to get around well enough on her own and then he'd take her there. But he wouldn't be going on his own. The last thing he needed was some kind of voodoo curse or something if he picked up the wrong stone.

As he drove around the next corner, he scanned the view ahead for signs of the truck. Maude had said it was next to the Quinn Valley Hotel & Spa, on an empty space of land. He spotted the hotel ahead, so drove toward it, finally noticing the taco truck surrounded by picnic tables and pergolas. It looked exactly how he would imagine a taco truck would look in a small town.

But what he wasn't prepared for, was the lineup of people standing there waiting to order a taco. He didn't think he'd ever seen a food truck this busy in the city. Obviously, with the warm weather, everyone had decided to get outside and enjoy some food.

He pulled into an empty parking space and

hopped out of his Jeep. If he hurried, he'd be able to beat the other carload of people that had just arrived. The smell of spicy taco meat filled the air and his stomach grumbled in excitement.

A woman with long brown hair at the front of the line turned after giving her order and her eyes slammed into his. He couldn't even tell what color they were, but something in them seemed to reach into his chest and squeeze. It wasn't just that she was drop-dead gorgeous. He'd seen and dated enough women in his life to recognize that there was something different about her, besides her stunningly beautiful face.

But no matter how hard he stared, he couldn't figure out what it was.

She obviously wasn't as affected as he'd been, because after doing one more quick scan of the line-up of people, she slowly walked toward an empty table to wait for her order. He tried to ignore the disappointment that she hadn't felt the same attraction as he had.

When he got to the front, he quickly placed the order his aunt had given him, turning his head slightly to look at the woman who sat with her back to him. What was it about her that was drawing him to her like a moth to a flame?

Groaning quietly, he chastised himself for having such cheesy thoughts. It's not like he'd never seen a pretty woman before. He was acting like a teenage boy, standing and staring at his crush while he tried to figure out how to approach her.

He'd been accused many times over the years of being a "player," and the accusation was one that had always bothered him. He'd dated a few women, but whenever things hadn't worked out, as they always seemed to inevitably do, a few of the scorned women had made statements about his character that had been damaging.

He'd tried shrugging it off, and acted like he didn't care, but the truth was that it *did* upset him. He wasn't the kind of man who would ever use a woman or lead her on, even if that was what some people believed about him. He just didn't believe in holding onto a relationship that wasn't working, simply with the hope that things would get better. So, he really didn't feel he should be blamed for the fact that he wasn't willing to settle for just anyone.

If that made him a "player," then he guessed that's what he was.

"Is that all for today?" Jared jumped as the man's voice, who had written down his order, interrupted his thoughts. Quickly turning his head back around, he smiled sheepishly.

"Sorry, I was a bit distracted. Yes, that's all. My aunt Maude sent me with the order and hopefully I've managed to get it all right."

The man was ringing up his order and smiled widely. "Oh, so you must be the nephew that was coming to stay with Maude. My grandma, Nellie, is one of her friends and they've all been talking about how nice it is that her nephew from the big city was coming here to look after her after her hip operation."

Jared nodded and laughed as the man mimicked his grandma. "I guess if you call Philadelphia the big city, then yes, that's me. And I know you have to be Ciran, the wonderful grandson who gave up his career as a lawyer to move home and follow his dream of running a taco truck." Now his voice did a perfect imitation of Maude's.

Ciran grinned as they shook their heads at how much the women in that group shared about each other's families. "That's me."

Jared pulled the money out of his wallet to pay, once more turning to look at the brunette waiting for her order. Her arms were crossed in front of her as she leaned against the table she was sitting at. She seemed to be lost in thought as she stared straight-ahead.

"I don't suppose you know who she is? I noticed you both seemed familiar with each other when she was ordering." When Ciran looked toward the woman he'd tilted his head toward, then back at him with a raised eyebrow, Jared's cheeks burned. He'd gone from feeling like a shy schoolboy to full-blown stalker.

"Well, that's Brooke Quinn. She's my wife's cousin. And also the granddaughter to one of your aunt's dearest friends, Gertrude." Jared was sure the last sentence was said as some kind of warning, in case he was having any ideas that would potentially harm the woman. Maude had filled him all in about the Quinn family and how close they all were.

"One of the famous Quinns. Maude tells me the town was founded by the Quinn family and they are all still living around here. I suspect I'll be meeting most of them over the time I'm here, with my aunt being connected so closely with the grandmother." He took his change from Ciran's outstretched hand and nodded before moving out of the way to let the group behind him place their order. With the amount of orders to fill, Jared expected to have a bit of a wait now until his was ready.

His legs were already taking him toward the woman—*Brooke*. Her name suited her. Now, if he could just keep his cool and not embarrass himself in front of her. Maybe the best way to be was up front and let her know he knew who she was already and see if he could join her.

"Hi, Brooke." Before he could tell her he was the nephew of one of her grandmother's friends, she whipped her head around and gave him a tentative smile, rendering him speechless.

If his friends could see him now, they'd be laughing at his complete lack of cool.

"You must be Jason." She stood up and put her hand out for him. When he wrapped his fingers around the warmth of her skin, he had to struggle to concentrate on what she was saying.

"Um, it's Jared." Her grandma must have already talked about him to her. He wondered how she was able to figure out it was him so quickly.

"Oh, I'm sorry. I must have remembered it wrong. I've already ordered my taco and am just waiting for it."

"I've just ordered mine too. Mind if I join you while we wait?"

Her eyebrows came together briefly, but then she

nodded and gestured to the other side of the picnic table. "Of course."

As he sat down, he tried not to make her uncomfortable by staring at her, but he just couldn't take his eyes off her face. She smiled, but there was something in her eyes that was holding back, and it made him want to find out why. He wanted to see her entire face light up with a smile.

"I was beginning to think I'd been stood up. I thought we'd arranged to meet here an hour ago, but I must have gotten the time wrong along with your name. I was just going to take my taco home with me. You can never be too sure when you arrange dates through those websites who will turn up," she said.

His breath caught as he realized what had happened. She was supposed to be meeting some guy named Jason and had thought he was him. But the fact that this Jason jerk had stood her up made his stomach curl in knots. How was he supposed to be the one to have to tell her?

Pushing his guilty conscience aside, he decided he wasn't. He couldn't do that to her. If it meant she'd keep that beautiful smile on her face, he'd pretend he was exactly who she thought he was. He wouldn't come right out and lie, and if she asked him, he would tell her the truth. It's not like he was doing anything wrong...

Maybe someday when they were old and gray, rocking in the chairs on their front porch, they would be able to look back at this and laugh.

CHAPTER THREE

Brooke glanced at the man across the table, noticing the strong jawline beneath the bright eyes staring back at her. Her heart did a little jump when he smiled but she reminded herself not to be taken in too quickly by a handsome face. Lord knew she'd run into enough pretty faces over the past few weeks who'd ended up being either complete jerks or mentally unstable.

She was definitely going to have to keep her guard up. Especially since this guy had already been an hour late and hadn't tried to apologize. When she'd said she thought they'd agreed to meet an hour earlier, he hadn't even said anything. And she knew she hadn't gotten the time wrong. Although she was still sure his name had been Jason...

"So, how long have you been in Quinn Valley? Your profile mentioned that you were new to town." She hated having to make small talk with strangers.

Just one more...then you don't ever have to do this again!

She reminded herself about the promise she'd made last night during the scene at the restaurant. This was the last date she was signing up for through that website. No more strange men trying to get a free diagnosis. No more awkward goodbyes at the end of the date as the man tried to find out if he could call her again, or worse yet, tried to kiss her.

"I haven't been here long."

Well, that was vague. Okay, maybe he didn't want to talk about it.

"Oh, well where did you come from?"

"Philadelphia. But I used to come here to visit family as a kid and always liked the area."

She laughed quietly and shrugged. "It is beautiful here, but I imagine it's a far cry from what you're used to in a city that big."

He looked around and shook his head. "Not really. When you live in a large city, you usually just hang around the same spots anyway. So not really that much different than a smaller town. Although I have to admit, I do enjoy how much slower life seems to move around here. I was never one to like the fast pace of everyone hurrying to make a dollar."

Well, so far, she had to admit he seemed more normal than anyone else she'd met online. But she wasn't letting her guard down yet. Especially since she was sure his profile had said he was an online stockbroker. Wouldn't that be exactly the opposite of the kind of lifestyle he'd just mentioned he preferred?

"So I guess with your job, you can work pretty much anywhere in the world. You wouldn't need to stay in the city. It must be an exciting career, though."

He stared at her for a moment, and she thought he was going to say something before he averted his eyes and looked down at the table briefly. She heard Ciran call out an order that was ready before hers.

Finally, he looked back up and nodded. "It is. I love doing what I do. And being able to work from anywhere makes it easy to travel to places whenever I'm needed."

This guy had to be holding something back. Something just didn't seem right. His answers were so vague that he could be talking about anything.

Her last shred of hope for this man being any different than all the others just slipped away.

Brooke didn't have time for any drama from a brooding man. Maybe she could fake suddenly feeling sick.

Just then, her cousin Roxane came over with her hands filled with wrapped food. "Here you go, Brooke. I just came down to grab a bite to sneak back up to my office, so Ciran asked me to drop this off for you on my way by." Roxie was looking at Jared intently as she handed one of the tacos to her. "And Ciran tells me you're Jared, Maude Butler's nephew. It's nice of you to come out here to help her while she recovers."

Brooke's heart sank to her feet as she suddenly realized what had just happened. Jared wasn't even the man she was supposed to be meeting, yet he'd let her believe he was! No wonder he'd been a bit confused in the beginning. Maude had told her about her nephew coming from the city to stay with her, but he certainly wasn't planning to live here and wouldn't have had a profile up on the SoulMates website.

She felt like a complete fool.

Glaring at him across the table, she waited while he talked with Roxane. Brooke wasn't the kind of woman to cause a scene, at least not in public, so she would wait until her cousin was gone so she wouldn't have to see her embarrassment.

Jared kept his eyes on Roxie's retreating back as she walked away, obviously aware he'd just been found out and hoping for some time to figure out what to say. When he finally looked at her, he put his hands up in front of himself. "Listen, I was going to tell you, but I didn't want you to think you'd been stood up by some loser who couldn't even bother to let you know he wasn't coming. It isn't my fault you got me mixed up and by the time I realized who you thought I was, I wasn't sure how to let you know the truth."

Her eyes squinted together in anger as she tried to control her words. She was a well-known family doctor in this town and she couldn't very well be carrying on like a raging lunatic in front of a taco stand.

"I would have expected you to have the decency to just tell me, so I wasn't wasting my time. Instead, you were sitting here laughing at me."

He shook his head adamantly. "No. I wasn't laughing at you. The simple truth is that I saw you, I wanted to come over and introduce myself, and you mistakenly thought I was someone else. I didn't come over here to intentionally lead you on. I just wanted to have the chance to talk to you."

She stood up, grabbing her purse off the seat with her empty hand while she flung her legs over the seat of the picnic table. "Well, you had the chance. If you'd just told me who you were to begin with, I would've talked to you anyway. But instead you decided to make a complete fool of me."

He was up now and raced over to her side, reaching out to take her arm. "I'm sorry. I really am. I should have told you as soon as I figured it out, but I didn't know how. I promise I'm not a bad guy. I just make stupid decisions sometimes."

He tried to offer her a sheepish smile, but she wasn't falling for it. Too many bad dates in the course of at least six weeks had played her out. She had no more to give anyone and she certainly wasn't going to be swayed by his charming smile.

He was no better than the rest of them she'd met.

And he was no better than the man who'd destroyed any chances she'd ever have of trusting another man again.

"Maybe next time you'll think twice before leaving your brain out of a decision that could end up making someone else feeling horrible. All I can say is that I'm glad I didn't have to waste any more of my time sitting here with you."

Ciran must have noticed something was up because he came over holding a bag that he held out to Jared. Ciran normally just called out the orders for people to come and pick them up, so the fact he was out here gave her some relief. "Here's the order for your aunt."

He stared at Jared for a moment, waiting until the man let go of her arm before looking back at her. "Everything okay?"

Brooke smiled sweetly while piercing Jared with her glare. "Everything is fine. I was just leaving to enjoy my taco in peace. There is absolutely no reason to sit and eat it here."

As she turned to walk away, she enjoyed a moment of joy as she saw that charming smile drop from his face.

Did it make her a bad doctor if there was a tiny part of her hoping he choked on his taco?

CHAPTER FOUR

"Can't I just skip family game night for once, and sit here wallowing in my self-pity? It's not like I ever win any of the games anyway." Brooke held a pillow clenched to her stomach while she stroked the soft fur of the orange cat snuggled up on her chest. "Besides, Winston is so comfy I'd hate to make him move."

Joel, her twin brother leaned against the doorway as his large, long-haired golden retriever Stanley pushed past him to jump on the couch beside her, sending Winston jumping away in a flurry of hissing and scratching. Stanley plopped his big head onto her lap and looked up at her with sad eyes, begging her to give him attention.

"See, even Stanley thinks it would be a good idea

to just stay here. You go on ahead, Stanley and I can have a quiet night eating ice cream and watching a movie."

"Brooke, just so you know, Robyn texted me this morning and told me about the less than stellar dates you had this weekend. So I know that's why you're sitting here feeling sorry for yourself. Honestly, I don't know what you expected from an online dating site. I don't know how you ever let our sisters talk you into that. Do you see either of them trying online dating? No—because even they know what a farce it would be."

She glared at Joel, letting her fingers move over the soft fur beneath them as they talked about Robyn and Vicki. Her younger sisters had helped her set up her profile and choose who she should respond to. It had seemed kind of fun in the beginning, hanging out with them and sharing in the excitement. That had changed pretty much after the first failed date, though.

"Well, considering the fact that they are younger than me, they still have better prospects around here than I do. And I don't exactly have the spare time to go places where I might find a date like they do." She rolled her eyes and shivered. "Anyway, I'm done with online dating. After my experience yesterday, I will never agree to a date with someone I don't know. The nerve of that man!"

She'd been fuming ever since yesterday afternoon and had sat up most of the night cursing Maude's nephew and wishing all kind of unseemly ailments on him. The worst part of it all was that she'd actually started to think he might have been different. Maybe he could have been the *one* normal date she'd managed to have in the past few weeks, months, and years since she'd had a boyfriend.

But no. He was the same. Or worse even. What kind of a guy let a woman believe he was the blind date she was supposed to meet?

She got angry again just thinking about it.

Joel pushed his fingers through his thick hair and sighed. "I agree, and if I see him, I assure you I will pummel him to within an inch of his life. Will that make you happy? Now, will you get off the couch and come with me? If we're late, I'm not taking the blame. Vicki already can't come because she's been called in to work, so Mom won't be impressed if her favorite son is late."

Every couple of weeks, sometimes more if everyone was available, her family would meet at her parents' house for Sunday supper and games. They'd always done it when they were kids living at home, and even as everyone had grown up and started to move out it had become a tradition to still go home and take part in the usual Sunday ritual.

When she and Joel had moved to the city to go to school, they'd soon found out how much they missed it when they couldn't take part.

"I'm sure Travis won't be late." She laughed as Joel pretended to scowl when she mentioned their younger brother. "Fine, I'll come. But I promise you that if Robyn or Mom or *anyone* mentions *anything* about me needing to try dating again, while giving me that sad, knowing look reserved for women who will surely die alone, I will scream."

"That's a bit dramatic, don't you think? No one thinks you'll die alone. I'm certain your twenty cats will all be by your side."

She glared at her brother as she threw one of the couch pillows at him. Stanley jumped up and chased it, excited that it might be time to play.

"I have *three* cats. And you're one to talk considering how many dogs and cats you have staying out at your place at any given time."

Joel was a vet, and he lived on an acreage in a small house behind his clinic, Quinn Valley Pawspital. But he also had kennels that housed animals while their families went on holidays, or strays who had no home and all other shelters and rescues were full. Brooke suspected many people took advantage of her brother's extremely big heart, knowing he couldn't say no to any animal in need, but he wouldn't listen to her. If anyone was going to die alone surrounded by animals, it would be Joel.

They made their way down the stairs and out to his truck. She lived in an apartment above her clinic in an old house she was still in the process of fixing up. It was turning out to be a bigger project than she'd imagined when she started, but thankfully she had a couple of people working out of the clinic now with her to help pay for everything. Her sister Robyn was a midwife, so she used a small room as an office, and Jill Caldwell was an obstetrician who did her consulting with patients here.

"I am coming over here next weekend and fixing these steps. You're going to end up falling and breaking your leg. Just because you're the only one who uses this side of the house doesn't mean you should just let everything fall apart back here."

She rolled her eyes at her brother as she opened the door to his old truck. It squeaked loudly as Stanley rushed past her to jump up into his spot beside Joel. He perched himself in the middle, staring straight-ahead out the window with his tongue hanging out of his mouth as he panted with excitement.

"I'm not letting everything fall apart. I have to spend my money where it's most needed and right now, that's making the clinic and the front of the house perfect. The rest can wait."

As they started to drive toward their parents' house, Brooke settled back into the comfy seat of her brother's truck. They all teased him about the old clunker he refused to get rid of, but the truth was it really did suit him. And she honestly couldn't see him driving anything else. Besides, Stanley had made the perfect indent in his part of the seat that could never be duplicated in another vehicle.

"So, I have to ask, and you're free to bite my head off if you want. But why are you suddenly so willing to put yourself out there and start dating again? Ever since..." Joel cleared his throat and glanced over at her nervously. "Well, you know. Since the stuff with Todd."

He quickly looked back out at the road ahead. "You've been so focused on your career and getting your clinic set up back here in Quinn Valley, it just didn't seem like finding yourself a boyfriend was high on your list of priorities."

Stanley turned his head and licked her cheek

before she had a chance to push him away. He always thought everyone would appreciate his affection and waited until their guard was down to shower them with his love.

"Yuck, Stanley stop that." She wiped at her face, pretending to be annoyed with the dog, even though she was secretly thankful for the extra moment to ignore her brother's question. But she knew he wouldn't drop it. Joel was annoying like that.

"Would it have anything to do with certain cousins all starting to find love and talk about weddings?" Joel snickered as he looked at her again, then quickly averted his eyes when she glared at him.

"Well, in case you've forgotten, we *are* two of the oldest cousins in the Quinn family. And we all know how much Grams and Gramps want to see us falling in love and living happily ever after like they did. Honestly, I think it's just about all Grams thinks about at the moment." She shrugged and leaned over to pet Stanley as they got closer to their parents.

At almost thirty-two, she and Joel were the oldest in their immediate family, however there were a few cousins who were older and still single. And even though she didn't want to admit it, it *had* been bothering her a bit finding out about some of the younger family members falling in love and talking marriage before she'd had her turn. She'd never really thought she was the type to care and had always said she'd be quite content to spend her life alone if she had to, as long as she had a career she loved.

But she guessed it must be something in the town water lately, or who knows what, that was making her start to question what she really wanted out of life. Maybe she *did* sometimes watch her cousins laughing and having fun with their new partners and secretly wished she could have that kind of love too.

The thought of someone to share her life with was starting to appeal to her a lot more than she'd have believed possible.

After she'd spent two years of her life, giving her heart and love to Todd, only to have him take it and stomp on it, it had taken her this long to be willing to try again. But it was obvious to her now that following the advice of her sisters to try online dating was *not* the way to do it.

They pulled up in front of their parents' house and Joel turned the truck off. Brooke looked at the front of the house they'd grown up in, with the large columns framing the wraparound porch. Whenever she came here, her heart felt calm and secure. Even though they always pretended to grumble about each other, her family was like no other. The closeness they had wasn't forced. They did everything together, and she always knew that no matter what happened in her life, there would always be four siblings and two parents cheering her on and prepared to do battle for her if needed.

Stanley was already vibrating with excitement knowing he was about to get attention from a whole new set of people.

"And, Joel?" He was just about to step out of his door, but he stopped and turned to look at her with a raised eyebrow.

"You should possibly start thinking about finding yourself someone too. I'm not the only one getting up there in age. In fact, if I remember correctly, you're a good ten minutes older than me."

She opened her door and hopped out, with Stanley right behind her as Joel shook his head and rolled his eyes. He caught up to her and put his arm around her shoulder as they walked up the front step. "No, thank you. I'm having enough fun watching you endure dating torture. No sense in us both suffering."

CHAPTER FIVE

"Be careful, Jared. The last thing I need is you ending up hurt too just before Christmas. I would never forgive myself if you were injured and had to miss going home."

Jared laughed as he reached up and clipped the strand of lights to the eave. "First of all, even if I do fall, I'm in much better shape than you, so it's unlikely I'll end up with a broken hip..." He grinned down at her as she huffed loudly in indignation. "And second, Mom and Dad are going to Mexico for Christmas so I'm probably just going to hang around here anyway, if that's okay with you."

He knew right away how happy she was to hear it as she clapped her hands together. "Oh, I'm sorry that your parents are leaving you alone at Christmas, but I'm not going to lie and say I'm not secretly a bit glad to know you'll be staying with me during the holidays."

Jared smiled to himself as he continued to work, peeking down at the older woman below, leaning against the rails on her deck. He hated to think of the Christmases she must have spent alone over the years. So many times, he would ask his mom if they could come to Quinn Valley to visit her during the holidays, but his parents just didn't think Christmas was that big of a deal. They'd rather take a holiday somewhere exotic than make any kind of important family memories.

His own grandmother had passed away when he was just a baby, so he had no memories of her. But Maude had immediately stepped in after her sister died to fill that role as needed, and Jared was grateful he'd had her in his life. She'd never had her own children, so her nieces and nephews, then great-nieces and great-nephews, became her whole world.

"Well, even if they weren't taking off somewhere, I'd probably have been staying with you anyway. There's something about this little town and how they celebrate Christmas that just seems incredibly appealing to me. Not to mention the fact I know you'd be apt to climb up the ladder to change a bulb or something crazy like that if I left you alone, so I'm not taking any chances."

"Jared! That's nonsense, and you know it. It only takes me falling from a ladder once to learn my lesson."

He climbed down and reached out for the bundle of lights she was busy trying to untangle for him. Her one arm in a cast was causing her some difficulties. "If you say so. Here, let me try getting these untangled. You go on in the house and warm up. There's no need for you to be out here hovering to make sure I'm doing everything right. I'll make sure your house is the most brightly lit up house on the block."

The weather had cooled down a lot in the past couple of days, and he was feeling the cold even through his heavy jacket. He knew Maude had to be freezing too, but she was far too stubborn to ever admit it.

"Hello, Maude. I'm surprised to see you outside when the ground is slippery like this."

Jared's head whipped around as that familiar voice reached his ears.

Brooke. What was she doing here?

"Oh my goodness, Brooke. I forgot you were coming by to check up on me today." Maude's cast hand flew up to her mouth as she clung to her cane with the other.

Brooke tipped her head slightly and laughed. "So, you're admitting that if you'd realized you might have been caught out here, you would have stayed inside?"

"Well, I have to get these lights up somehow. You know the judging for the Christmas yard displays will be starting in a couple of weeks and I want to make sure mine looks perfect."

Jared tried not to let himself stare, but his cheeks burned when Brooke turned her head and caught him looking.

"Jared, this is Brooke Quinn. She's a family physician here in town and the granddaughter of a dear friend of mine. Brooke, this is my nephew, Jared Webber. He's the one I was telling you about who was coming to stay with me."

She was his aunt's doctor?

He put his hand out and nodded his head. Brooke slowly put her own hand out, but he was sure if his aunt hadn't been watching she would have refused. As they shook, he silently cursed the gloves they were both wearing that prevented him from being about to feel her skin.

"Doctor Quinn." He chuckled quietly as a grin spread across his face. "Like, as in Doctor Quinn..."

She quickly let go of his hand and put hers up, cutting him off before he could continue. "Don't even say it. Everyone always thinks they are the first ones to realize that I am, in fact, Doctor Quinn, Medicine Woman. But I assure you, I hear it every single day. So, unless you're Sully and coming to sweep me up onto the back of a horse, don't even *think* about calling me that."

"I had no idea you were a doctor." He couldn't help the smile that was spread across his face at seeing her again.

She just shrugged and crossed her arms in front of her as she pulled her collar a bit tighter. "You never asked. Besides, I thought you would have found everything else out about me when you asked to know my name."

He could see she was still angry about what had happened, and he didn't blame her. He just hoped he could figure out a way to make things right with her.

Maude looked at Brooke, then back to him in confusion. "You two have met already?"

Brooke raised her eyebrows and watched him

with interest to see how he would explain their meeting to his aunt.

"Oh, yes, Maude. Didn't Jared tell you?"

He cringed slightly as he met his aunt's confused stare. "Well, we did meet briefly the other day when I went to get your tacos. There was a slight misunderstanding and I'm afraid I might have acted like a bit of a horse's backside..."

Maude's eyes widened, and her mouth dropped open in shock.

"Jared Webber, you better not have!"

"I promise you, as soon as she will allow it, I plan to make it up to her."

Maude turned to look at Brooke who was grinning with enjoyment at his discomfort. "Brooke, I'm so sorry. I don't even want to know what he did. But let me assure you, he will be making it up to you. Tomorrow night, I insist that he take you out for a meal and show you how a proper gentleman is supposed to act."

Now it was Jared's turn to grin. Brooke's mouth opened but she wasn't saying anything. He could see she wasn't the type of person who might cause a scene by refusing to let the nephew of her patient take her out on a date to apologize. She didn't want to hurt Maude's feelings.

He couldn't have planned a more perfect moment. If he'd asked her, he had no doubt in his mind she'd have flat out refused.

Tilting his head slightly as he continued to work at untangling the lights, he smiled widely at her. "It's the least I could do, Brooke. I promise you, I'll be on my absolute best behavior. It would mean a great deal to my aunt to see me make things right."

Her eyes squinted slightly as she faced him again. "Well, I don't know, Maude. I'm so busy right now with Christmas coming up and everything. I have to get out to the tree farm and pick my tree up this week, then all of the decorating at the clinic. I've got so much going on."

"Oh, please, Brooke. I feel just terrible that my nephew might have acted in any way to upset you. If you could just give him a chance to show you, he is actually a nice young man." Maude glared at him. "Even if he does sometimes act like the back end of a farm animal."

"Let me take you out to help pick your tree up. That way, I'm not interfering with all of the many things you have going on and it will give us the chance to get to know each other properly."

"That's a perfect idea. What do you say, Brooke?" Maude looked up at Brooke expectantly.

Normally, Jared would be mortified that his aunt was practically begging a woman to go on a date with him, but right now he could pick Maude up and kiss her for helping him. Brooke couldn't say no even if she wanted to.

Giving them both a forced smile, Brooke finally nodded. "Okay, he can help me pick up my Christmas tree." She didn't sound thrilled about it but at least she'd said yes.

Maude reached over and patted her arm. "Thank you, dear. And don't you worry about a thing. If he even so much as looks at you the wrong way, I want you to tell me. Of course, he will also be paying for everything." She gave him a stern look. "Including your Christmas tree."

He opened his mouth to mention that a tree would probably cost a lot more than a normal date would, but quickly shut it when his aunt continued to glare at him, daring him to argue. He was a smart man.

Brooke smiled and put her hand under his aunt's elbow to start walking her into the house. "I'll take that offer. Now, let's get you inside so I can take a look at you. It looks like Jared has things under control out here."

He stood watching them slowly make their way

along the deck toward the front door. Brooke kept her hand on his aunt's arm, keeping her steady so she wouldn't slip. When she turned her head back and caught him staring again, his breath got stuck in his throat.

What was it about this woman that had him tied up in more knots than the lights he was holding in his hands?

Whatever it was, he was going to enjoy spending the time untangling it.

CHAPTER SIX

"Won't your tree be completely dried out by the time Christmas actually gets here?"

Brooke smiled to herself as they made their way down the next row of trees. The farm was located just outside of town with what seemed like miles and miles of trees planted in perfect rows. Each year it rotated the area that was to be used as the trees matured, and then new trees would be planted in their place. Some years, Brooke would just go with her family to get her tree at the ranch, but she also liked to support the local businesses too. Besides, since she wasn't paying for her tree this year, she may as well make the most of it and get a perfectly grown one.

"It doesn't if you keep it watered. And I don't know why you think the beginning of December is too early to decorate. Everyone in Quinn Valley gets into the Christmas spirit early. I'm actually late getting started this year."

Jared was walking beside her, the snow beneath their boots crunching as they walked up the row. The sun reflected off the whiteness of the ground, sparkling off the branches of the trees that were covered in a light hoarfrost. She pulled her neck warmer up a bit higher as the chill tried to sneak in under the warm fabric.

"It's still the first week of December. When do you normally start?" He looked at her incredulously.

"I like to have my tree up by the first. My whole family is like that. Even my brothers, although they try to act like they're scrooges, they don't actually fool anyone. Ever since I can remember, Mom has made such a big deal over Christmas that I guess it just rubbed off on the rest of us."

She watched Jared as he gave a small shrug, then turned back to investigating each tree with interest. "What about this one? It looks good."

Brooke moved over closer and looked the tree up and down. It was the fifth one Jared had pointed out so far, but she could see she still had a lot to teach him about picking out a Christmas tree. "Well, this one is better than the last one you picked. But see how when you stand back here, some of the branches are a bit shorter on this side than the other?"

She tried not to laugh out loud as she watched him step back and tilt his head slightly to get a better look at the tree.

He'd arrived a bit early to pick her up but had waited at the clinic while she saw the last of her patients. And on the drive out here, he'd been a perfect gentleman and had assured her she would get to meet the real Jared, not the one who had left such a bad first impression. So far, she'd actually been enjoying herself with him, but she wasn't prepared to let him completely off the hook for that first meeting.

"I think you're just messing with me now. There's nothing wrong with this tree. Each branch is perfectly shaped." He squinted his eyes slightly as he faced her with a wide smile.

She pretended to think it over, stepping back to get another look. The truth was, she normally would have just picked the first one they'd found. Her tree never ended up looking that good anyway. After the first day of being decorated beautifully, her cats usually made sure it didn't look anything like that by the time Christmas arrived. So having the perfect tree really didn't make that much of a difference.

But she was enjoying dragging Jared through the trees in search of that tree she had led him to believe would make Christmas complete. Then watching his confusion every time he thought he'd found one, only to be told it wasn't quite right. She knew she should still be mad at him over what he'd done at their first meeting but after spending time with him today she realized he really wasn't that bad of a guy. Holding a grudge wasn't going to prove anything.

"You realize it's going to be dark soon and then it will be impossible to find a tree." He crossed his arms in front of his chest and waited for her to decide. "I don't know about you, but I'm nearly frozen right through. Once the sun is gone, we will probably die out here from hypothermia."

"Well, I guess it will have to do then." She laughed as he rolled his eyes and nodded.

"Good. I'll go find that man we talked to earlier who said he'd cut it for us." As he walked away, she let her eyes follow him. He was tall, and his shoulders were broad beneath his heavy coat. She felt a small twinge of guilt knowing she'd kept him out walking around in the cold longer than necessary. He'd offered to get the tree up to her apartment for her and get it standing, so she would offer him some hot chocolate or something to warm him up.

Her stomach did a somersault as she realized that she'd be taking a man to her apartment. She hadn't known any of the men she'd gone on a date with enough to even invite them upstairs. But she somehow sensed that he wasn't the kind of man to take advantage of the situation. Plus, his aunt was friends with her Grams, so if he even tried anything, Brooke knew they'd both have his hide.

She was determined not to let her fears and mistrust ruin the fun she'd had with him over the past couple of hours.

"OKAY, LIFT YOUR SIDE DOWN CAREFULLY."

Brooke followed his instructions, slowly letting the side she was holding slide from the roof of his Jeep.

"No, be careful! Hold it up!" His voice was muffled as he struggled to hold up the massive tree that was threatening to knock her to the ground. She should have never let him pick a tree this big. Now she was beginning to wonder if it would even fit into her apartment.

As she tried to hold on to it while he undid the final strap, she could feel it starting to slip. "Jared!" she hollered loudly in fear as she realized she was about to be crushed to death by a giant Christmas tree. But before it could land on her, he'd pushed her out of the way and taken the brunt of the trunk swinging from the roof. It hit him hard on the head before knocking him to the ground as the tree fell beside him. Pine needles sprayed everywhere, covering the snow around them.

"Jared, are you all right?" She quickly kneeled down in the snow to check on him.

Blood was already pouring from a large gash just above his eye. He reached up to wipe at the blood as he tried to sit up.

"Here, let me help you. Put your arm around my shoulder." She took his hand and wrapped his arm over her shoulders as they stood. He held his other hand over the cut to try and stop the bleeding that was leaving a trail of bright red on the snow.

"I'm fine, Brooke. It's just a cut. I've had worse." He sounded a bit dazed, and she worried that he might have a concussion.

"No, it's not just a cut. I'm taking you into the clinic and cleaning it up. You'll likely need stitches."

His eyes opened wide and he shook his head adamantly. "Absolutely not. No way am I letting you stick any needles in my head." He stopped walking and refused to move.

She turned her head to the side and looked up at him with an eyebrow raised. "You aren't afraid of needles, are you?"

He scoffed and shook his head again as he tried to stand on his own. "Of course not. I'm a grown man. I'm just not fond of the idea of anyone sticking me with needles or sewing me up when I'm not entirely sure that person isn't still angry with me."

She wasn't sure she believed him. He was trying to protest just a bit too much. "Well, first of all, I'm a doctor, so it would be against the law for me to act on any personal feelings when dealing with a patient." She'd placed an arm behind his back to help steady him, so she tugged slightly to get him walking again before he bled out right behind her clinic. It probably wouldn't be a great way to build trust with any patients coming in tomorrow if she just let him die back here.

"And second of all, I'm not angry. You've proven

to be an all right guy today, so I can let go of your less than stellar first impression."

He stopped again and looked down at her with a grin on his face. "Does this mean you'll let me take you on a proper date? And hopefully one that won't have us freezing the entire time, only to end with one of us suffering from serious head trauma?"

"I don't know. It's not really ethical to date a patient. And once I get you inside and sew you back up, that's what you'll be." She laughed at the stunned look on his face.

"Well then I am refusing medical treatment. I really don't want you to see how un-masculine I am around needles anyway."

She rolled her eyes and tugged again. "Fine, I will go out with you again on the condition you let me take care of that cut. It really is bad, and you need to get it fixed."

"Can't you just use some strong Band-Aids or something?"

By now they were at the back door to the clinic, so she let go of him to reach into her purse for her keys. He leaned against her slightly while he waited.

"No, Jared. You need stitches. I promise the needle won't hurt a bit." She felt like she was having to convince a child that everything would be okay.

"And if you're good, maybe I'll even give you a sticker."

He clenched his jaw tight and looked inside the open door as though he was motivating himself to go into battle. Finally, he took a step inside.

"If I survive this, please promise me that I will get to pick what we do for our next date."

CHAPTER SEVEN

"Are you sure you're feeling up to this? You aren't showing any symptoms of a concussion, but I know your head has to be hurting at least a bit."

Jared opened the door to the restaurant and let Brooke go in ahead of him. He would never admit how much his head was actually still throbbing. If he did, he knew she would insist they go home so he could rest. There was no way he was passing up this chance to be out on a real date with her, even if he did end up passing out in his salad over dinner.

It would be worth it.

Yesterday at the Christmas tree farm, he'd found himself smiling and laughing more than he had in a long time. Once she'd let down her guard a bit and not focused on his stupidity from the day at the taco truck, they had actually been able to have a lot of fun together. She was a bit picky about finding the perfect tree, but he hadn't really minded because it meant he could spend more time with her. His fingers had been almost completely frozen off, and then he got clobbered with a Christmas tree, but other than that, it had been a perfect day.

He hoped tonight would end up without any injury.

"I'm fine. Quit trying to get out of your date with me. A deal is a deal. I didn't even cry or pass out when you stuck that ridiculously long needle into my forehead, or when you proceeded to repeatedly stab me with that hook while you sewed me back up. So, you owe me."

Her laughter made his heart skip a beat. *How could one woman have such an effect on a man?*

"Well, I'd say that since I was the one doing the stitching, technically you owe me, but we won't argue about that. You were a very good boy and didn't fuss too much when I jabbed you, so I guess I can follow through on my end of the bargain."

"Thank you." He grinned as he let her lead them to a table in the restaurant. She'd mentioned that it was owned by her cousins, and he'd asked if they should go somewhere else, so they couldn't be interrupted. But she'd insisted it wouldn't be that bad, even though he already had a feeling they were going to have more sets of eyes on them all night than he'd like. However, Maude had told him that Brooke hadn't been having much luck with dates lately, so he suspected she wanted to be somewhere she felt safe.

He could give her that.

It didn't matter to him where they went, as long as he got to spend the evening with her.

As soon as they sat down, a young waitress came rushing over. "Hi, Brooke. I'm glad to see your back." The woman looked at him warily, as though she was somehow expecting him to show he had another head or something.

"Ivy, this is Jared. He's not a date from the Internet. He's Maude's nephew who came to stay with her." He put his hand out to the waitress who obviously knew Brooke well. "Jared, this is my cousin Ivy."

"Oh, well then hopefully you won't need rescuing tonight." Ivy laughed at her own joke and took their drink order.

Once she left, he grinned across the table at Brooke. Her cheeks were a bright shade of red as she rolled her eyes in Ivy's direction.

"She's exaggerating. I've had a few dates over the

past couple of weeks that resulted in me needing some assistance to get away from, but I'd hardly say they had to *rescue* me."

"Well I hope she's right. I'd hate to think you'd need rescuing from a date with me. However, I will be on my guard now for anything suspicious that might require you to suddenly have to leave."

They sat and talked while they waited for their meal to arrive, and she was laughing as she shared the details of some of the dates she'd been on. He was sympathetic and even shared a couple of dating stories he'd experienced in the past that he said he'd rather try to forget.

In the hour since they'd arrived, he'd met three more cousins who he knew were now keeping a watchful eye on them. Ryder and Maggie owned the restaurant and bar, and he'd noticed them looking their way more than once. And another cousin named Andrew had come in with his girlfriend Rachel. They'd both quickly came over to introduce themselves to him and it seemed that Rachel and Brooke might be good friends.

He really hoped that the next time he took her out, she'd agree to go somewhere with a little less company.

And he already knew he'd be asking to take her

out again. He'd never met anyone who did what she did to him. He was enjoying every moment with her and he didn't intend to let her get away. Even though he'd only known her now for about a week, he knew she was different.

"So, we've talked about how horrible dating is. You know just about everything about me, along with my family and what I do for a living. When are you going to share more about yourself? All I know really is that you don't make a good first impression and you're a bit accident-prone."

Their plates arrived, and they thanked Ivy, who looked back and forth between them, probably waiting to see if Brooke was going to give some kind of signal to imply she needed to be rescued. Or, more likely, she was trying to decide if he was some kind of dangerous criminal adorning a giant black goose-egg on his head with stitches stretching across it. Everyone they'd met tonight had stared at his forehead and he could tell they were dying to find out about it, but he'd gotten a bit of enjoyment out of leaving them to wonder what had happened.

It made him feel a bit more mysterious. And to be completely honest, he really didn't want them all to know he'd been almost knocked unconscious by a Christmas tree. He was hoping to make a better first impression on her family than he'd managed with her.

"What would you like to know? There's not too much interesting to know about me. I grew up in Philadelphia with parents who believed working and putting money away for retirement was more important than doing anything with their children. And one sister who moved to New York as soon as she was able to drive. So you can see my family isn't quite as extensive as yours."

"What about Maude?" Brooke took a bite of her pot roast and closed her eyes briefly as she started to chew. "Oh, this is good."

He had to smile at how much she was truly enjoying her meal. It was refreshing to be with someone so honest and uninhibited. Too many times women would put on an act, sometimes even pretending to just want a small salad thinking that would impress him.

"Maude is my great-aunt. I used to come and stay with her a lot when I was a kid, but I guess over the years as I grew up, I didn't make the effort to see her as much as I should have. She's more like a grandma to me than an aunt, and when I heard she'd hurt herself I realized time was passing by and she wasn't getting any younger. I needed to make more time for her before it was too late."

He stopped and stared at Brooke for a moment, wondering why he'd just shared stuff with her he hadn't even really thought about himself until now. She just smiled and took another bite; completely unaware he had just completely opened up to her like that.

"When we first met, you mentioned that your job allowed you to be able to move anywhere you wanted." She made a face at him as she continued. "Of course, at the time, I thought you were some kind of online stockbroker like it said in your profile."

He cringed slightly as she brought that up again. At least she wasn't mad anymore.

"I'm an author. I write crime fiction."

She opened her eyes wide with excitement. "You're really an author? I think I do remember your aunt mentioning something about you being a writer, but I kind of assumed that just meant you were between jobs. You know, the whole struggling writer thing."

He laughed and shook his head as he took a sip of water. "Well, I do actually make a living from my books, so I guess I'm not struggling too badly. I find it's sometimes easier not to mention what I do simply because everyone does automatically assume I just don't have a job."

They laughed and continued their meal, and he was finding himself getting pulled even farther into her eyes every time she looked at him. Just being around her made him feel happy.

When it was time to pay, Brooke excused herself to go to the washroom before they left. He went up to the counter at the bar to give them his credit card instead of waiting for Ivy to come to the table. The restaurant was so busy he didn't want to make any extra work for her.

Another woman stood near the counter talking to Maggie. She turned when he got there and smiled at him. "So, you're, Jared? I hear you're out on a date with Brooke. I think you're the first one she's actually managed to stay through the whole meal with."

"Jared, this is Renae, another one of our cousins." Ivy walked up behind him, taking his bill and punching it into the till.

"Another cousin. I wonder if it's possible to go anywhere in Quinn Valley without running into a Quinn cousin."

Renae shook her head emphatically. "No, I doubt it."

Ivy handed him back his card and smiled at him

tiredly. "I'm sorry if I didn't get back to you guys much. It is so busy in here tonight." Suddenly, she gasped as she stared across the restaurant before quickly looking at Renae. Renae followed her gaze and cringed.

"Oh no."

Jared immediately noticed Brooke coming back toward them at the same time as a couple walked into the restaurant. She had to go around them to get past and he could see the exact moment all color drained from her face.

"What's going on? Who is that?" His pulse was already racing as he sensed something wasn't right.

"That's Todd. Her ex. With his new wife."

She'd briefly mentioned an ex, but he couldn't remember what had happened. Or, if she'd even really told him.

Renae looked at him with her face crumpled like she was genuinely in pain. "He dumped her two days before their wedding and ran off to elope with her matron of honor. It's the kind of thing you would only ever believe happened in the movies, but it happened to her. She lost her fiancé to her best friend and they didn't even have the decency to tell her to her face. They just ran off and let her live with the humiliation."

Ivy was shaking her head, staring at the confrontation that was about to happen across the floor. "It was two years ago, and they at least didn't come back to town to rub her nose in it. Well, until now. I'd heard they'd moved back here but was hoping I was wrong. I never liked her friend Amanda. She always had to compete with Brooke and couldn't stand to let her have anything she didn't. Now she'll be flaunting her marriage in her face."

Jared couldn't listen to anymore. His legs were already moving toward Brooke, whose panic-stricken eyes briefly met his just as he got to them.

"Sorry I took so long, sweetheart. Are you ready to go?" He leaned over and planted a kiss right on her lips, before putting his arm around her shoulders and turning to face the couple. He pretended to just notice them while Brooke stood staring at him in shock, obviously unsure what was going on.

But he didn't care. He wasn't going to let her stand here and be humiliated on her own.

CHAPTER EIGHT

"Oh, I hadn't heard you were seeing anyone, Brooke." Her ex-best friend looked Jared up and down slowly, much like someone would do when searching for that perfect piece of meat to buy in a store. Brooke tried to calm her racing heart while her brain searched for words.

Thankfully, Jared filled the silence for her. He put his hand out to Amanda, sweetly smiling at her. What was he up to? "Yes, I'm Brooke's boyfriend, Jared Webber. We've been seeing each other for..." He turned his head to look at her, pretending to think about how long they'd been dating.

Brooke was still confused, trying to figure out why he was doing this.

"I'm not exactly sure, but it's been awhile now."

Why was he lying for her? Her eyes moved past him and saw Ivy and Renae watching them. He'd been over there paying, so they'd obviously filled him in on all the sordid details of her epic breakup. A weight lifted from her shoulders as she realized what he was doing. If she had to face her ex and his new wife, she wasn't going to have to do it alone.

"Um…yes, a while. Jared, this is Amanda and Todd…" She didn't know what to call them. Her backstabbing ex-best friend? Her ex-fiancé who'd ended up being a cheating, lying jerk?

Todd was looking at her with a strange expression, then he faced Jared as he shook his hand. Jared's other arm was still planted firmly around her shoulders.

"It's nice to meet you. You're looking well, Brooke." Todd had turned his eyes back to her, and for a brief moment she remembered the love she'd felt for this man. But it was soon wiped away, replaced with the memory of what he'd done to her. She could never have truly loved him because she obviously had never really known the real man he was.

This had to be the most uncomfortable conversation she'd ever had to endure. Especially when

Amanda lifted her eyes to scowl at Todd, obviously thinking his gaze was lingering a bit too long on Brooke.

Jared's arm squeezed a bit tighter, giving her a boost of strength she desperately needed. "Thank you. I've been doing great." She wanted to tell Todd how glad she was she'd found out what kind of man he was before she'd said her vows, but she wasn't sure this was the right time or place.

"So, you've just stayed living here in Quinn Valley, Brooke? After all that time getting your doctor degree, and you come back to stay in a little town like this. It's such a shame."

Amanda's voice was like fingernails on a chalkboard. How had she ever believed this woman was a friend? Brooke realized how naive she'd always been, only seeing the good in people even when her entire family let her know how much they'd never trusted Amanda.

Brooke had always been a bit of an introvert, content to just be at home reading and away from crowds. She didn't do well with groups of strangers, and Amanda had been that outgoing friend who'd taken her under her wing and brought her out of her shell. But now that Brooke looked back, she realized Amanda just liked being with her because it made herself look better. She was the blonde, popular, good-looking party girl while Brooke had always been the quiet brunette that made Amanda stand out even more.

But once Brooke moved away and studied to become a doctor, that made Amanda jealous. Suddenly, she wasn't the one people were noticing. When Brooke had come home to visit and ended up dating Todd, a wealthy real estate agent, Amanda just couldn't take it. She'd made sure Brooke couldn't have something she didn't have.

"I'm still living in Quinn Valley, with my own practice."

"Yes, lucky for me, Brooke is the kind of woman who doesn't need to put on any act about who she is to impress anyone. She provides a much-needed service in this town, and I couldn't be more proud. It's funny how some women just seem to have it all together, you know? That's Brooke. She would never have to flaunt anything she has because she knows no one can compete with her. I feel sorry for anyone who would even think they could try." He was smiling at her as though he was completely in love with her and just had to brag, but she could see the sparkle in his eye as he gave Amanda the subtle cut-down.

He turned back to the other couple, not giving them any chance to speak again. "Sorry for rambling on like that. We'll let you get on with your date."

Todd's eyes were still on hers, looking like he didn't quite believe she could have possibly moved on. Did he seriously think he was that much of a catch that she couldn't have ever found anyone else?

Smiling sweetly at Jared, she put her arm around his back and let him lead her away. "It was nice seeing you both." She hoped she didn't get struck down by lightning when they walked outside for speaking that outright lie.

When the cold air outside touched her cheeks, she let go of a deep breath she hadn't even realized she'd been holding. "That was just about the most awkward situation I've ever been in. Well, I guess except for all those phone calls I had to make to wedding guests to tell them they didn't have to come. Or when I had to return the gifts we'd already received and opened. Those times weren't fun either."

She was trying to make light of the situation, even though the truth was, seeing them here tonight—together—had deflated her. It wasn't like she hadn't known they were married. And it *had* been over two years since everything happened.

But seeing them for the first time since then was hard.

Jared let go of her shoulders and stopped, taking her hand and turning him to face her. "I'm sorry you had to go through that, Brooke. I wish we'd have left sooner."

She shrugged weakly. "It was going to happen sooner or later. I'm just glad you were here with me to help get me out of there."

He held onto her hand in the quiet of the parking lot as snow gently drifted down between them. The streetlights gave off an orange glow that reflected off the newly fallen flakes on the ground. She found herself unable to look away from his gaze as he watched her.

"I'm glad you didn't marry him."

Such a simple statement, but she could tell he was completely serious. She laughed softly and nodded her head in agreement. "Well, I'm glad too. Better to find out a man is a complete pig before he gets the ring on your finger." Again, she tried to act nonchalant, hoping he wouldn't ever see how much it had hurt her at the time.

He lifted his hand and brushed her hair back, his fingers barely touching the skin on her cheek. "You deserve better than him. Someone who can appreciate you and who would never hurt you like that. It was all I could do not to knock him to the ground when I heard what he'd done to you. But I didn't think you'd ever agree to a second date with me if I did something like that to embarrass you in public." He smiled widely, taking away some of the seriousness of his words.

His hand dropped down to his side and for a moment, he looked completely vulnerable and unsure of himself. Her pulse picked up speed again as she suddenly found herself desperately hoping he would kiss her.

Where had that come from?

"We should probably get going. But I want you to know that I had a wonderful time tonight. It was a refreshing change to not have to try sneaking out of a date."

He laughed and nodded. "I'm glad to hear that. I had fun too. And was quite relieved not to end up needing any kind of medical attention throughout the entire evening."

As they got into his Jeep, Brooke peeked over at him. The strangest thing had happened tonight, and she wasn't quite sure what to make of it. Somehow, instead of feeling the longing she'd expected she would feel when she saw Todd again, he'd already been forgotten.

Right now, all she could think about was Jared. And she knew it was silly, but how she had enjoyed that brief moment of him belonging to her.

CHAPTER NINE

"Are you really sure you need another set of lights to go around it? Honestly, you've got more stuff on this tree than I've seen on the one at Rockefeller Center in New York." Jared tried to push the string of lights into the branches somewhere, hoping he could find an empty spot. "Although I have to say this tree you picked out is almost the same size as the ones they have there, so I can understand the need for a lot of decorations."

Brooke peeked around from the other side of the tree with a big smile on her face. "You picked the tree out, remember?" She hung a red bow on the branch she was working on, then looked back at him. "I've always wanted to see that tree in New York. I've always imagined Christmas in New York City must be so magical, with all of the decorations everywhere."

His heart did a little flip as he watched her get a dreamy look in her eyes. "Well, some day you should go. I've been to New York more times than I can count, and I hadn't really paid much attention to the decorations that were up at this time of year. And I'd just always kind of thought of the tree at Rockefeller Center as a big tree that must take forever to decorate and cost a fortune to run all the lights on."

She shook her head as she rolled her eyes and reached down into the box for another ornament. "Men. Can't appreciate something as beautiful as that."

His hands stopped moving as he bit his tongue, not wanting to make a fool of himself. Brooke carried on placing more ornaments one at a time onto each branch, completely unaware that he was struggling not to blurt out that he *could* appreciate something—or someone—who was beautiful. He was sure if she was standing beside that enormous tree in New York, she'd steal all attention away from it.

But he couldn't tell her that without it sounding like some kind of cheesy, practiced pickup line. He knew she'd had some rough dates over the past while, so he really didn't want to scare her off. He was enjoying being with Brooke and talking to her. Even yesterday, although they hadn't met up or done anything, they'd been texting all day and just having fun getting to know each other.

"I'm glad you agreed to come help me decorate my tree. I still feel bad that it injured you, so I'm hoping this will help you to get over any anger you might have toward it."

He laughed and shook his head. "I doubt it. Every time I look at this tree, all I can think about is the fact that it tried to kill me."

"I still don't quite know how I'll get my angel on the top. We might have to cut some of it off." She looked up at the branches they'd had to fold over in order to get the tree to fit into the room.

He knew the tree was way too big when they'd picked it out, but she'd insisted it would be fine. But after he'd been stitched up the other night, and they'd finished bringing the tree upstairs, she'd had to admit he was right. The tree was enormous in this small room.

Suddenly, the tree shook for what had to be at least the tenth time since they'd started decorating it as one of her many cats jumped up and began its climb to the top. A gray face poked out from halfway, it's eyes wide with excitement as it tugged at a loose piece of garland.

"Kiki! Get out of there!" Brooke reached in and pulled the cat into her arms, giving it a little scratch under the chin before setting it down. "This is why I can't have nice things. And exactly why my tree will end up looking like it's been through a tornado long before Christmas ever gets here. I always say the reason I have so much Christmas spirit is because I literally have to re-decorate my tree every couple of days."

He could see that by tomorrow, the tree wasn't going to look anywhere near as good as it was now. The cats were hovering around, poking their noses into boxes, stealing garland and playing with it, not to mention trying to sneak into the branches every five minutes.

"Why do you have such strange names for your cats? Most people use things like Tiger, or Miss Kitty." He'd never had any pets growing up because his parents hadn't thought it was necessary. They thought animals were just an extra burden that they didn't have time for.

"Well they aren't really strange names. All my cats are rescues my brother Joel had taken in. Casanova was named that because he was what you might call a bit of a ladies' man. He always had a herd of female cats following him around and he loved it. And Winston just looks like a Winston so that's why I called him that. But Kiki wouldn't answer to anything when Joel first took her in and she was really skittish. Whenever one of the workers would go to call the cats, they realized the only time she came was when they called, *here Kitty Kitty*, really fast. Since we really didn't want her to be called *Kitty Kitty* we shortened it to Kiki which sounds the same."

He laughed and shook his head. "Well I stand corrected then. All of those names are perfectly suited."

Brooks cheeks started to burn and she smiled sheepishly. "Sorry. I guess that was a bit more information than you needed. Now I *do* sound like a crazy cat lady."

"Not at all. I think it's sweet that you have rescued these cats and given them a home. Someday I want to get a pet, probably a dog, though. I don't think I'm much of a cat person. They seem a little bit too high strung for me."

The tree shook again, and the lights clinked together as another cat made an attempt to get to the top of the tree without being discovered. They obviously weren't very smart animals. Why not wait until there was no one around who could catch them? Or at least try to do it quieter so they might not notice?

This time, Casanova stuck his head out. At least he thought it was Casanova. He looked pretty chill and proud of himself, so Jared figured it had to be him.

"Winston! Get out of that tree!"

Jared just continued to wrap the last bit of lights onto the tree and laughed. He hoped he'd get to spend enough time around here that eventually he'd be able to figure out which name belonged to which cat.

Where had that thought come from? Ever since he'd met Brooke, he'd been thinking long-term thoughts instead of the usual *she's nice but not someone I could ever see spending my life with* thoughts. He had to admit it made him a bit nervous. What if she wasn't thinking the same way?

Of course she wasn't. They barely knew each other.

After all, he'd only known her for a week and for the first part of that, he was sure she would've rather never seen him again. She was just so different from anyone he'd ever met that he was having a hard time figuring out what was happening.

He'd heard of love at first sight, but never believed in it. And he knew for a fact, that hadn't been the case for her. He cringed to himself as he remembered that first meeting again. No, he didn't think this was love at first sight. But it was definitely a case of completely knocked off his feet at first sight.

Now, he just needed to catch her up to where he was.

CHAPTER TEN

"Are you sure you're feeling up to this? It's not too late to back out. Things might be a bit crazier in there than you're used to." Jared had never really talked much about his own family, except for telling her briefly about his parents and a sister. Brooke had the impression their family wasn't very close, and that career and other things were more important than spending time together. Nothing at all like her own family.

Now they were sitting in front of her parents' house about to go inside. Once he did that, she was afraid he might be tempted to turn and run away as fast as he could go.

"Your mom was nice enough to invite me over for supper with everyone, so I'm not going to say no to that. Besides, how much crazier can it be than spending the afternoon setting up a giant Christmas tree in a space smaller than a closet, while three cats did their best to destroy it?" He reached to open his door and grinned at her as he stepped out.

"Trust me, when my family gets playing board games, things can get a bit out of control." She didn't want to admit how nervous she was for him to meet everyone. It wasn't that she didn't think they'd like him. Jared had proven to be a very likeable guy, once she'd gotten to know him. But the truth was, she hadn't brought anyone home since Todd. Was it too soon to introduce them to him? I mean, she didn't really know him that well, did she? They hadn't even had a first kiss! Well, not a proper one. What if things didn't work out?

Brooke! Can't you just let yourself enjoy being with him and let things happen on their own without analyzing and worrying about everything?

Chastising herself, she opened her own door and joined him in front of the Jeep. "Are you sure? Everyone is here today, so it's going to be loud."

Since Vicki hadn't been able to make it last weekend, her mom had called while they were setting up the tree to invite her for supper again this weekend, saying everyone would be able to make it today.

When she'd declined and said she had company, of course her mom had been ecstatic and invited Jared too.

Everyone was already here, and Brooke's stomach clenched in knots. Looking at Jared, he was grinning at her like he didn't have a care in the world. He was just about to meet a bunch of strangers. Wasn't he the least bit nervous?

"Come on, I'm sure it won't be that bad." He reached out and took her hand, the warmth of his skin radiating through her thin gloves. It felt so natural to have him hold her hand like this and she found herself hoping he'd never let go.

"So this is why you didn't need a ride with me and Stanley. Mom said you already had an offer for a ride, but I couldn't think who it would be. Now I see you've let some strange man bring you here."

Brooke cringed as Joel opened the door and stood in the doorway with his arms crossed, pretending he was insulted. "Very funny, Joel. This is Jared, the man I'd mentioned helped me pick out my tree and who took me for supper on Friday night. Jared, this is my twin brother, Joel. Although I really don't like having to admit that."

Joel stuck his hand out to Jared. "Oh, right. I do remember you mentioning him. Isn't he also the one you met that day at the taco truck? What was it you said to me after that?" He put his fingers up to his lips as he pretended to think while she wished a giant hole would open up and pull her under the porch. "Oh right! I think I was supposed to pummel him or something along those lines for the indignity he inflicted on you. Although by the look of that shiner on his eye, I'd say someone already beat me to it." Joel squinted and pretended to cringe as he examined the large gash over Jared's eye.

Brooke punched her brother hard on the arm. "Will you just get out of the way, so we can get inside? No wonder I don't ever want to bring anyone home to meet you people." She turned to look at Jared, afraid he'd be mad that they'd been talking about him after their first meeting. "I'm sorry. Of all the people you had to meet first, it had to be him. He thinks he's funny, but no matter how much we tell him the truth, he doesn't believe us."

"Brooke, I'm so sorry. I tried to get here before Joel could, but I was up to my elbows in the sink before I even realized you'd pulled up."

Brooke leaned in to give her mom a quick hug, then stepped back to introduce them.

"I'm so glad you agreed to join us for supper,

Jared. Now we will actually be able to have an even amount of people on our teams for charades."

Trust her mom to be more excited about teams for their games than the fact her oldest daughter had brought a man over for supper.

"Irene, will you let them in the house before you start organizing us into teams?" Her dad put his hand out to Jared. "My name is Harold. I hear you're staying with Maude to look after things while she's recovering. That's awful good of you to do that. Especially since I'm sure the lifestyle is a bit different here than you're used to in the city."

"Well she's always been good to me over the years, so it's the least I could do for her. Besides, I like it here in Quinn Valley, so it really isn't any hardship for me." When Jared turned his head and smiled at her, his eyes full of warmth, her heart jumped.

Jared handed his coat to her mom and they followed her father into the living room where everyone stopped talking and looked at them with wide grins. Why had she ever agreed to let Jared come here? It would have been so much easier to make him meet her family one at a time. Instead, he was seeing how immature they all were as they sat staring. She expected them to start singing,

"*Brooke and Jared sitting in a tree...*" any moment now.

Robyn was the first to jump up and race over. "So you're Jared. Brooke has told me all about you."

Brooke actually thought flames might break out on her cheeks. "Well, I've hardly told you *all* about him, Robyn. I mentioned we'd gone out a couple of times." Why had she ever confided anything to her siblings? She was pretty sure any chance of another date with him was slipping away every time someone in this house opened their mouth.

Vicki came over too, offering them both a sympathetic smile. "I'm sorry for our family, Jared. Unfortunately, everyone here tends to be a bit unstable and when you bring a newcomer into the mix, I'm afraid some of the people around us don't know how to act properly." Brooke mouthed a thank-you to her youngest sister, who she had just decided was her favorite sibling.

"So, what exactly happened to your face? Did my sister do that to you?" Brooke cringed as Travis came over for his introduction. They hadn't even been in the house for five minutes and she'd wished the ground would open up and swallow her at least a hundred times.

"Actually, she did." Jared laughed and put his

hands up to protect himself as she gasped and turned to face him. "Well, not directly. And to be fair she did fix me up after, so I can't really be mad."

"I didn't do that! It isn't my fault the tree fell and hit you."

Travis and Joel both laughed loudly, obviously enjoying her discomfort knowing it might have been somewhat her fault that Jared had been hurt. Her brothers could be annoying enough on a regular day but now that they obviously sensed the testosterone levelling out in the room, instead of the usual woman majority, they were all going to thump each other on the backs and celebrate their manliness.

Thankfully, her mom interrupted by clapping her hands and announced the team divisions for the first round of charades. "Since we have an even number tonight, we'll be playing boys against the girls."

Brooke's eyes met Jared's and she could see the sparkle from where she stood. With a wide grin she went to sit beside her sister, prepared for battle. She'd never wanted to win anything more in her life.

CHAPTER ELEVEN

They pulled up behind her house and Jared shut the engine off. Brooke stared up at the window to her apartment, smiling when she noticed the lights on her tree had turned on. "Looks like the timer you set up for me worked."

Jared leaned forward to get a better look. "You sound surprised. I'm not just good looks you know. I can be quite handy when needed."

"I will never doubt you again." When they'd been setting the timer, she'd been unconvinced he knew what he was doing as he tried to adjust the dials. But he'd insisted that since his aunt had made him put up enough lights to be able to safely land a plane on her yard, he was quite sure he knew how to set one little tree timer.

It was snowing again outside, and the lights she'd hung in the back reflected against the whiteness. He opened his door and stepped out, his boots crunching onto the ground. As she reached for her door and pulled the handle, he hurried around to pull it open.

"Brooke, can you just let me try to be a gentleman here and open your door for you? Honestly, you're making it very difficult for me to make a good impression."

She rolled her eyes and took the offer of his outstretched hand. "I've been opening car doors on my own for many years, Jared. I can manage just fine. However, I do appreciate your attempts."

He didn't let go of her hand as he closed the door behind her. They stood facing each other in the quiet of the night with the wet flakes landing on their skin.

"Well then how can I ever woo you properly if you won't let me do gentlemanly things? Surely there is something I could do to impress you." His voice was low, sending shivers through her chest.

She was trying to concentrate as his thumb began to move around in circles on her hand. She wished she'd never put her gloves back on, so she could feel the heat of his skin.

"Woo me?" She laughed at his choice of words. "If I didn't know better, I'd almost think you've been reading some of those historical romance books your aunt has piled up around her house."

He shrugged and grinned widely. "I might have flipped through them a bit to see what I could do to sweep you off your feet. I've never dated a woman like you before, Brooke." He swallowed and held his eyes on hers.

"What if I told you that you were doing a pretty good job of taking my feet out from under me and you really don't need to try so hard?" She had never been able to speak so openly with anyone before, even when she'd been with Todd. But around Jared, she somehow just knew she could be herself and didn't have to hold anything back. Her heart pounded in her chest as she waited for him to say something.

Suddenly, his smile grew even wider and he reached into his pocket. A moment of complete panic overtook her. Surely, he wasn't about to propose to her! They'd hardly even spent any time together and hadn't even kissed! Well, except for that kiss when he was rescuing her in front of Todd, but that didn't count.

What would she say?

But before she could turn and run, he held up a

small piece of green Christmas decoration. *Was that...?*

"Mistletoe." His eyebrows moved up and down quickly as he held it above them. "I stole it from Aunt Maude's big box of decorations. She won't even miss it. But I thought it might come in handy tonight if I couldn't think of any other way to kiss you."

Afraid to breathe in case she somehow broke the spell, she could only stand still as his hand came up to lightly brush her cheek, then moved around her neck to pull her close. His other hand still held the mistletoe above her head, but once he had her pulled up against him, it wrapped around her back. His head slowly lowered, his lips touching hers softly. But as soon as they met, her heart started beating double time and the world around her started to spin.

She brought her own arms up around his shoulders and held on for dear life as her legs turned to Jell-O beneath her. Just when she was sure she would collapse on the ground in front of him, he finally pulled back and stared at her with wide eyes. His shoulders moved up and down quickly, matching her own ragged breathing.

"What just happened?"

His voice rumbled deep in his chest, vibrating against her own that was still held up next to him.

She swallowed and shook her head slowly. "I don't know." There was no sense in pretending she hadn't felt it too. She'd never been kissed so completely and held so tenderly in her life. Now, here she stood in Jared's arms with just the glow of the Christmas lights around them and the softly falling snow, and she felt like the world had just been tipped upside-down.

His fingers came up and gently traced lines along her chin and behind her ear. Everywhere he touched left a trail of warmth even with the chill of the night air blowing onto her skin. His eyes followed his fingers as they moved. "Brooke, I'm glad you gave me another chance. I knew the moment I saw you at that taco truck there was just something different about you. I kind of feel like I'm in one of those silly romantic Christmas movies that Maude has been making me watch with her every day this week."

She smiled and tipped her head back slightly as his fingers started to trail along her neck. "I think your aunt Maude is a good influence on you. Here you are reading romance novels and watching sappy movies. Maybe you'll have to give up writing crime fiction books and start writing romance yourself."

He pretended to think about it, then laughed. "The only romance story I am interested in right now is ours."

Her eyes held his for a moment. "So, are we having a romance story then?" She wasn't sure what to think of what was happening between them, but she knew it was more than just a couple of dates she'd had and would move on after they'd spent some time together. It just felt different. And she realized with a shock that she'd never even felt like this with Todd.

But it scared her to be feeling so much for him already. How much did she really know about him? He never really talked about his life, other than mentioning he was an author and a bit about his family. Yet, she felt like she knew so much about him just from spending time with him.

"I'd like to believe we are. And I plan to make it the best story ever. Now, if only I could think of something else I could do so that you'd see how much you want to keep me around. What can a simple man like me offer to a beautiful woman doctor like you?"

She could tell he was trying to joke with her, but she suspected there was a hint of real insecurity behind the words. She knew as a doctor, people were sometimes intimidated around her. In fact, it was one of the reasons she had few friends outside her cousins and siblings. And Amanda had torn away any shred of trust she had for other people, so making friends wasn't easy for her. Other than Rachel, her cousin's girlfriend, there wasn't really anyone who wasn't family who she trusted.

"Well, I hear you've become quite good at putting up Christmas decorations. This woman doctor could really use a hand decorating the front of the clinic, so she doesn't look like a scrooge compared to the rest of the businesses in town." She grinned widely as he cringed slightly and pretended to shake his head dramatically.

"No way. I'm done with Christmas decorations. Besides, I'm pretty sure Maude has used up the last of any stock that would be available in Quinn Valley." He held his arms firmly around her back now, not letting her go. "Surely you could think of something else—anything else—I could do to impress you."

She leaned her head against his shoulder, letting his fingers move up to play with her hair. "There's nothing that would impress me more than seeing a man up a ladder decorating for Christmas." She smiled to herself, enjoying the chance to stand here in his arms like this and be able to tease with him like she'd known him forever.

He sighed loudly, then kissed the top of her head. "Fine. If that's what my lady wants, that's what she'll get. I will spend every spare moment I have decorating her place so she has the best display in town."

She pulled back and grinned up at him. "Your lady? You really have been reading those books of your aunt's, haven't you?" She laughed and shook her head. "Why shouldn't I be surprised?"

He grinned widely as they pulled apart and he put his arm around her shoulders to lead her to her door. "I'm merely an author studying other works to build on my craft. I can't help it if I'm picking up some extra tips along the way." He looked down at her with a dramatic expression. "So, don't be alarmed if you see me riding in to save the day on the back of a white stallion."

She rolled her eyes and laughed. But somehow, she could almost picture Jared doing just that.

CHAPTER TWELVE

"So, you're the guy who's been seeing Brooke. Man, at the rate my family has been succumbing to this whole growing up and settling down bug, there won't be many single ones left by this time next year. Luckily I'm smart enough to keep that from happening to myself."

Jared laughed with Brooke's cousin Dusty as he spoke about keeping himself away from any kind of commitment with a woman. Brooke had warned him about her chiropractor cousin who worked in the office, Joint Ventures, with her brother Travis and how he was probably the biggest flirt in town.

Maude was in Travis's office having her physical therapy appointment to start getting the range of motion back in her hip now that it was healing. So

Jared had been left in the waiting room with Dusty while he talked to the receptionist, Amy, a kind older lady who rolled her eyes at Dusty.

"Dusty McIver, one of these days you'll find a woman who will steal your heart, just you wait. And when that happens, I can't wait to see your face." She laughed at the thought and went back to typing something on her computer.

"Never going to happen, Amy." Dusty shook his head adamantly.

"Well, I'd hardly say Brooke and I are at the settling down stage yet. Although I'll admit I'm hopeful that's in our future. And I used to think a lot like you, Dusty, until I met Brooke. So never say never."

Jared smiled to himself as he looked back down at the magazine he held. He wasn't really reading it anyway, more just flipping through the pages to kill time while he waited for his aunt. But when Dusty had come out from his last client, he'd shown a great deal of interest in Jared, obviously wanting to make sure he was a suitable match for his cousin. Jared was beginning to realize that there was nowhere they could go in Quinn Valley without running into a cousin, an aunt, or a fifth-uncle-once-removed, who were looking out for each other. The Quinns were everywhere.

Over the past couple of weeks, he'd spent just about every day with Brooke when they could. He'd wait and pick her up after work to go for dinner, or to a movie, or even to just sit on the couch with her while they watched something on TV and talked. He'd never felt so relaxed and comfortable with a woman in his life like he was with Brooke. They laughed, told stories about their pasts and shared secrets. She'd opened up to him about how hard it had been after Todd had hurt and humiliated her, and how she'd had a difficult time letting herself get back out there again. That dating website had ended up being a complete nightmare for her. But he'd told her he was kind of glad she'd wasted her time going on dates with all of those duds so that when she met him, the bar really hadn't been set too high for him to jump over.

The bell over the door jingled, announcing a new arrival so they all lifted their eyes to see who had come in. "Oh, Dusty, I hope you have time to squeeze me in. I've hurt my back somehow and I need you to fix it." Amanda, Brooke's ex-friend and wife to her ex-boyfriend sauntered into the waiting room in a flurry of perfume and blonde curls. She hadn't even noticed him sitting there as she strode toward the counter. "Todd is waiting in the car because he said he didn't think he'd be welcome in here, but I told him he was being silly. I know things will be a bit awkward for a while but now that we're back in town I hope everyone can just move on."

Dusty leaned against a wall behind the counter and crossed his arms over his chest. "No, he's right. He wouldn't have been welcome in here. I'm surprised you feel that you'd be welcomed with open arms, though."

Her mouth dropped open and she stopped moving. "Well, I've known you for years. I've known all of the Quinns, so I just assumed since you were a chiropractor now, that you'd welcome the business from an old friend."

Dusty laughed and shook his head. "Not any friend of mine."

Amanda looked over and noticed Jared sitting there. "Oh, I see. You've got Brooke's new boyfriend in here and it wouldn't look good for you to be nice to the *enemy*. I think you all need to just get over the fact that Todd chose me. I can't help it that we fell in love and I was more suited to him than she ever was. Todd is a wealthy businessman who would have quickly grown bored with Brooke. You all should be thanking me that I helped him to realize he needed something more than a mousy, quiet girl who'd rather sit at home with her cats, than go out socializing and networking."

Jared stood up slowly and walked toward Amanda, shaking as he fought against the anger that was threatening to explode from him. It wouldn't be easy to keep wooing Brooke from a jail cell, so he refrained from putting his hands around the woman's neck like he wanted to do.

"Well, that's something I can agree with. Dusty, we really should be thanking Amanda. I mean, if not for her, Brooke would have ended up married to a flaky swine who obviously can't be trusted. It's obvious he can't think for himself and can be easily swayed by another pretty face. Thankfully, Brooke won't ever have to be married to a man who we know would never be able to remain faithful to one woman."

Amanda's face was red, and her eyes squinted as she clenched her fists at her sides.

"Who do you think you are, talking to me like that? From what I hear, you're nothing more than some kind of writer who most likely can't even pay your own bills. That's why you're living with your aunt. You're exactly the kind of man I'd imagine Brooke to end up with."

"Do you have any idea who you're talking to, young lady? Honestly, I'm so glad you and Todd ended up together. You're perfectly suited for each other." Maude came marching out of Travis's office as fast as her limp would allow, lifting her cane from the floor and pointing it at Amanda when she got in front of her. "My nephew is perfect for Brooke, and it's not just because he's a famous author. It's because he's a kind man who will treat Brooke the way she should be."

Jared kept his jaw clenched tight. Why did Maude always have to make him out to be more than he was?

Amanda scoffed and shook her head. "Famous author. Who's he supposed to be, Stephan King?"

Maude leaned closer and Jared was afraid his elderly aunt was about to knock Amanda to the ground. "No, he's J.D. Webber. You might have heard of him."

He heard both Travis and Dusty give a small gasp as Amanda's mouth dropped open. "J.D. Webber?" Her voice wasn't as shrill as it had been before. "The crime writer?"

"Not that it should make any difference, considering a few seconds ago you were acting like I was nothing more than a speck of dirt on your shoe, but yes, J.D. Webber the crime writer."

Amanda's lips slowly turned up into a dazzling smile as she came over in front of him. "Oh my goodness, I never even realized. I guess I've never really seen what you look like, so you can understand my mistake. I can't believe we have a real author living here in Quinn Valley. Why didn't Brooke mention anything about it when we met the other night?"

The woman's entire demeanor had changed as though now that she recognized his name, she needed to treat him nicer. Well, he didn't care if she started oozing rainbows and sunshine, he wasn't going to be taken in by her fake kindness.

"Probably because it isn't really that big of a deal. I'd like to think Brooke just likes me for who I am, and not because of a name she might have heard of before."

Amanda watched him for a moment, then gave a laugh that stood his hair on end. "She doesn't realize who you are, does she? You never told her." She laughed again and shook her head as she walked toward the doorway. "Well, isn't she going to be in for a shock when she finds out. Let me know how that goes, her liking you for who you are and not because of your name thing."

Jared had always thought of himself as a calm person and not really someone who could hurt another human being, even though he did write dramatic crime fiction.

But right now, as he watched Amanda walk away, so sure she had some kind of juicy gossip, he was already plotting a character just like her in his next book, so he could have her meet a gruesome demise. And he couldn't wait to write that chapter.

CHAPTER THIRTEEN

"I'm so sorry, Brooke. I didn't even think about the name when I booked it." Brooke looked down at the file in her hand for her next patient. *Todd Ewings*. Of all the doctors in town, why did he need to come to her?

"It's fine, Melody. It isn't your fault. You weren't even working here when all that stuff happened with Todd, so you wouldn't have known." Her receptionist had only been with her for the past year since she'd set up her own clinic, and Brooke could never be mad at her anyway. She was just about the sweetest girl in the world and would never do anything to hurt anyone.

"I know, but I still feel terrible. I would have told

him you weren't taking any new patients or something if I'd known."

Robyn came out of her office across the small corridor and joined them. "What's all the whispering about?"

"It would appear Todd has some medical ailment he needs me to look at."

Robyn's mouth formed an "o" and then her eyes pulled together in anger. "He's got a lot of nerve coming to you for anything. I'm going out there to tell him he's not welcome in this office."

Brooke rolled her eyes at her sister's temper. "No, Robyn, you don't need to do that. We have a waiting room full of patients that don't need to have a soap opera moment played out in front of them. Just forget it. I can handle Todd just fine."

"Well don't let him play you, Brooke. Honestly, he doesn't even deserve a minute of your time. At the very least, I hope you'll tell him he requires a shot and you use the largest needle you can find."

"I'll do my best to ensure he suffers some kind of pain while he's in there." She had to laugh at her sister and how dramatic she always was. "You can send him in, Melody."

Brooke walked into her office and waited, giving herself a few seconds to compose herself and to stop her hands from shaking. Other than that brief meeting in the restaurant with Jared, she hadn't spoken to Todd since she'd received the text to say he wasn't marrying her and that he'd fallen for Amanda.

"Hello, Brooke. Thank you for agreeing to see me."

Her breath caught as that familiar voice reached her ears. She looked up and smiled, nodding her head for him to sit in the chair next to her desk. "Hi, Todd. What can I do for you today?"

She wasn't about to sit here and pretend to make happy small talk with him like she might with any other patient. No, she was just going to get to the point and get him out of here as quick as she could.

He laughed quietly and gave her that smile that used to melt her heart. Right now, all it did was make her want to slap his face. But she didn't think it would look good to put that in his medical records under any treatments she'd performed while he was there.

"Aren't you even going to ask how I am? I've thought about you so much, even more since seeing you that night at Quinn's. I was so shocked to see you, I'm afraid I didn't really get the chance to say much to you."

"Well, I will ask how you are from a medical

standpoint, but other than that, I don't really care. I'm seeing you as my patient, nothing more than that. So if you came here to chat about our past, you may as well leave right now."

Todd's smile slowly faded, and he looked down at his hands. "I'm so sorry, Brooke. I know I messed things up badly, and I should have told you in person. But Amanda just seemed to have me tied up in some kind of knot and I wasn't thinking straight. I need you to forgive me."

Brooke took a deep breath and leaned back in her chair. It was obvious he wasn't here for anything medical related. "If that's what you need, then fine. I can forgive you. But that doesn't change anything. I will never want to be around you or Amanda ever again. I've moved on with my life and I'm finally happy again. I won't let you ruin that."

"Are you really happy, Brooke? I know ever since the day I left, all I've done is think about what could have been with you. I would give everything I have if I could go back and do things different." His eyes lifted to hers, trying to pull her into them like he always used to do. "Please tell me it's not too late. Let me have another chance."

Her stomach twisted as she struggled with what to say.

"Todd, how can you even think there would ever be another chance for us? I might have been bowled over by your good looks and charm while we were dating, and maybe wasn't able to see through to who you really are, but I'm not the same person you walked away from two years ago. There is nothing...*nothing*...you could say that would ever make me want to try again with someone like you. And besides that, you're married now, or have you already forgotten that? I think you should leave, Todd."

"I'm sorry. I didn't mean to come in here and blurt everything out like that. I really didn't want to upset you." He thrust his fingers through his thick hair, leaving it in a mess that she used to find charming.

"I mean it, Todd. I'm over you, and in fact, I'm so glad we didn't end up getting married. I was able to spend some time discovering my own strength and finding out that I didn't need any man to make my life complete. And then when I was ready, I found someone who has shown me what respect is, and how a woman should be treated."

"Right, I forgot about your new boyfriend. What's his name again?"

Brooke didn't like talking about Jared to Todd. It was none of his business.

"Oh yes, Jared Webber. Or J.D. Webber as his fans know him."

J.D. Webber? Brooke didn't read crime fiction, but she'd heard of J.D. Webber. He was almost a household name. What was Todd talking about? For some reason, he believed he had something that would hurt her image of Jared, but she wasn't about to let Todd think he had the upper hand with her or that she'd be angry with Jared.

"Listen, Amanda mentioned that she was talking to Jared the other day and that it turns out he is actually a well-known author, but she also said he hadn't even bothered to tell you who he really is. I'm just worried about you. I still love you, and I hope you realize that sometimes people aren't who you think they are. I know I don't deserve another chance, but maybe just don't throw me away so quickly without thinking about it first."

"Get out of my office, Todd. I don't ever want to see your face again. One thing Jared has over you is the fact that he would at least be man enough to break up with a woman to her face—not send her a text two days before her wedding to say he'd decided he was in love with her best friend. You have a lot of nerve coming in here and trying to trash talk him under the pretense that you just care about my well-being. You never cared about anyone's well-being other than your own." She stood up, shaking with anger, finally letting out all the words she'd always wanted to say to him.

"And now, you think you can waltz in here and try to make me doubt what I have with another man because you can't stand the fact that I'm not still just sitting around pining over you." She pointed her finger at his chest as he stood up to face her, his eyes wide in shock that this quiet, little mousy girl was actually speaking to him like this. She knew there were likely people in the waiting room who could hear every word, but she was past caring.

"Well, let me tell you something. I wouldn't go back to you if you were the only man on earth who had a water hose and I was on fire. I would rather spend the rest of my life tied to a pole while wild birds pecked my eyes out than to *ever* spend another minute with you."

Todd's cheeks were bright red as he turned to open the door. "Fine. But a word of advice. You might think your new boyfriend is a step up from me but let me assure you that all men are the same. If you think any man can spend his life with just one woman, you're crazy. And I'd think if he was someone you could trust, he'd have told you the truth about who he was in the first place."

He slammed the door behind him and she sunk into her chair, swallowing hard against the dryness in her throat. Her heart thumped so hard she could hear it echoing in the small room.

She sat in her chair, shaking as she looked out the window to the parking lot. Todd strode out to his car confidently, putting on the perfect show of being completely together. No one would ever see Todd Ewings rattled because he wasn't the type of man to care enough. How had she never noticed that about him before now?

But he'd left her rattled. The words he'd spoken about Jared being a famous author who hadn't told her the truth replayed over and over in her mind. Why would he have kept that from her? It's not like it would have made any difference. She wasn't the type to care for someone because of their name. She wanted to believe the best of him, but now she wasn't so sure.

Todd had placed enough of a worry in her heart that Brooke knew it would eat at her until she found out the truth. What if he was right?

What if no man could be trusted?

CHAPTER FOURTEEN

"Uh-oh, looks like Maude is going to have some competition with this one. Where on earth did they find an inflatable reindeer that big? Looks like I might have to make a trip into Lewiston this weekend to get a few more things for her yard."

Jared stopped his Jeep in front of the house they were driving past, taking note of the decorations. They'd been driving around the town, sipping on hot chocolate they'd picked up at Fresh Brew while they got into the Christmas spirit looking at all the lights. The town judging would happen next week, before Christmas, so he still had time to add some more to Maude's.

Brooke laughed and shook her head. "A month ago you couldn't understand why anyone would waste so much time decorating, and you thought too many lights would look awful. Yet, here you are now saying you need more. Between the decorating you've been doing at Maude's, and then at my clinic, I'd have thought you'd be done." She looked at him for a moment, then down at the cup in her hands. "Besides, it likely isn't giving you much time to write. You must have deadlines you need to meet." She lifted her eyes back up and he sensed she wanted to say more but was holding back.

She'd been quiet ever since he'd picked her up earlier and he wasn't sure what was going on. He'd hoped taking her to look at the lights would cheer her up a bit, and he had a surprise he wanted to show her. Maybe he should just head there now.

"Well, that's the good thing about being a writer. I can set my own schedules. I do have a book that needs to be at the editor by the middle of January, but that's still lots of time. Right now, I'd rather spend my time with you." He pulled away and drove toward the spot he'd been spending the past few days getting ready. He peeked back over at Brooke who was staring at her cup again as though she was afraid it was going to fall from her hands.

"Brooke, do you want to tell me what's bothering you? I thought you would love looking at all the lights tonight, and I have something I wanted to show you. But I can't stand seeing you like this. Have I done something to upset you?" He racked his brain trying to remember if he'd said something wrong or maybe if he'd forgotten something he was supposed to do, but there was nothing he could think of.

She sighed and shrugged slowly. "I'm sorry. It's just been a long day and I'm a bit tired, I guess."

He didn't believe her for a minute, but he hoped once she saw his surprise, she'd smile. As he came around the next bend, he grinned in anticipation. "OK, you need to close your eyes."

"What? Why are you making me close my eyes?"

"Just do it. Don't argue."

Brooke's eyebrows pulled together in suspicion, but she finally closed her eyes.

"I know you're peeking, Brooke. Put your head down into your hands."

She huffed loudly in indignation as she opened her eyes and glared at him. "Uh, I wasn't peeking, Jared."

He just pointed with his hand for her to cover her eyes and put her head down in her hands.

"Fine. But you better not be planning anything that's going to embarrass me."

"I'm hurt that you think I'd do something like

that. I promise, you'll like it." He drove around the corner, immediately seeing the reflection of the lights in front of them. He glanced over at her to make sure she wasn't peeking, then stopped and shut off the engine. "Now, keep your head down until I come around and get you out."

He kept his eyes on her as he jumped out and raced around to her door. "OK, now keep your head in your hands and step out. I'll help you."

"Jared, this is ridiculous. Just let me lift my head up. I promise I'll keep my eyes closed."

"Nope, I don't trust you. Here, just step out and I'll hold your arm." He helped her get out of the Jeep and led her around to the front, turning her to face his surprise. "All right, you can look now."

His eyes stayed on her face as she lifted it to look at the massive tree in front of her. It was lit with so many lights, the orange glow reflected on her skin. Her mouth dropped open and her hands came back up to cover it in surprise. She stood for what seemed like forever, just staring and taking it in before finally letting her hands fall back down and turning to face him.

His chest squeezed with emotion as he noticed the tears in her eyes.

"Jared, it's beautiful! But I don't understand..."

"Well, I know you said you've always wanted to see the big tree at Rockefeller Center but since I can't really take you there right now and leave Maude alone, I thought maybe I'd try to bring it to you." He looked up at the tree that stood in front of the Quinn Valley Senior Center and shrugged, suddenly feeling a bit embarrassed. Most men would get their girlfriends jewelry or chocolate, but no, Jared Webber got his, a giant Christmas tree.

"I know it's a bit silly, but I was talking with Joel the other day when he stopped by the clinic about how I'd like to do something... I was outside hanging your lights and we got talking, and well, I just thought this would be nice." He'd planned this big speech about how much he cared about her and just wanted to make her happy, and now he was having trouble putting two words together.

Brooke slowly walked toward the tree, her eyes wide and a smile covering her face. *That* was what he'd wanted to see.

"It's obviously not as big as the one in New York, and some day I'd really like to take you there for real." *Stop talking Jared. She can see it isn't as big as the one in New York without you telling her!*

"No, it's perfect!" She grinned over at him and

turned, taking his hands. "And the seniors in the home will be able to see it from their rooms."

He nodded, glad she was happy with the tree. "When Joel and I started planning and talking about it, I wasn't really sure where we could put it. It's not like there is much open space right now downtown, and I didn't think I should put it in front of your clinic or people might not even be able to find you behind it. Vicki happened to come along when we were discussing it and she said the home where she works had a huge empty space in front and it would be perfect there. That way, people from town could come out to see it and the seniors would be able to enjoy it too. Some of them who can get around on their own have been coming out each day to help us get it decorated and they've been loving it. Especially when they found out I was putting it up for you."

Brooke threw her arms around his shoulders almost knocking him to the ground. "This is so wonderful. I can't believe you did this for me. Thank you."

He held her tight and pressed his lips to her hair. "Well, I'll admit I might have been doing it for selfish reasons too. I was kind of hoping you'd end up in my arms after seeing it, so my plan has worked perfectly." He smiled at her as she pulled back and looked up at him. Her cheeks were red from the chill of the air and her eyelashes had a hint of white on them.

"First you use mistletoe to get me to kiss you, and now a giant tree to get me in your arms. I do believe you've become a softie for Christmas, Jared."

He shrugged, bringing his hand up over them to show that he was still carrying the mistletoe. "I'm just a resourceful man."

She laughed when she saw it, then leaned in to press her lips to his.

After their first kiss that night, Jared was sure he'd fallen in love with Brooke, but he wasn't really sure how to tell her. He'd kissed her many times since then and every time, he knew he was falling even harder.

But this one—this time, standing here beside the lights of this enormous tree—he knew he was gone. Brooke had his heart and somehow, he was going to find a way to let her know.

CHAPTER FIFTEEN

"I'm so glad to see that things are working out between you and Maude's nephew. Who would have thought the two of you would ever end up together?" Grandma Gertie reached over and patted Brooke's hand, nodding her head while she looked at her with a twinkle in her eye. Brooke knew she'd never be able to prove it, but she somehow thought her grandmother had some kind of hand in her being with Jared. And Grandma Gertie would be properly offended if she even asked her for the truth.

"Well, Grams, we've been dating for a few weeks now but that doesn't mean he's the one I'm going to be spending my life with. So don't get yourself too worked up. Remember how well things worked out for me before."

Her eyes scanned the crowd to see where Jared had ended up, and she spotted him standing by the bar talking to her dad. The family Christmas party was well underway at Quinn's, and Brooke was sure this year everyone had shown up. Even her cousin Andrew was here, and other than Thanksgiving, he hadn't been coming to family functions for a long time. She was glad to have Jared with her this year, and as she watched him, he turned his head as though he knew she was looking at him and their eyes met. Holding her breath, she listened to the echo of her pounding heart as she realized just how important he'd become to her in such a short time. When he smiled at her, warmth spread through her entire body.

"Brooke Quinn, honestly, I'm tired of you using that as an excuse for everything." Her head spun back around to face her grandma and her eyebrows came together in confusion.

"Excuse me, Grams? What are you talking about?" After staring at Jared, Brooke honestly couldn't remember what they'd even been discussing before.

"You're always throwing it out about what happened with Todd. Now I admit, that was a pretty awful situation to have to go through, but you can't keep bringing that up and believing it will happen to you again. It's time to let it go and just be happy going forward with a man who won't do something like that to you." Grams clucked her tongue and looked over at Jared. "Besides, I can tell the way that man looks at you that he would move the world for you, if you just asked him. He would never hurt you the way that other pot-bellied swine did."

Brooke laughed in shock at her grandma's name for Todd.

Grams just shrugged. "What? I never liked that boy. Trust me, I have better names for him, but they aren't said out loud by a lady. I hate to say it, but I was so glad when I heard the wedding was off. I never believed he was the one who would make you happy for the rest of your life. It was never meant to be."

Her cousin Renae came over, leaning down to kiss Grams on the cheek before sitting down at the table with them. "I love all of our family get-togethers, but this Christmas one is always my favorite. Everyone is in such a joyful mood, and it just feels like we all really appreciate each other. I know it's silly since we all still live around town and see each other all the time, but being together like this for

Christmas just makes me happy, you know what I mean?"

"I do. I feel it too. Even if we did just all get together a few weeks ago for Thanksgiving." The three women laughed, knowing full well that no one outside of the Quinn family could ever understand how close they all were. Getting together like this wasn't even hard to do, because once a date was set, everyone made sure they could come because they genuinely enjoyed being together.

Brooke's eyes moved around the restaurant full of Quinn family and friends. She spotted Maude sitting at a table talking to one of Gram's other friends and as she looked, Maude lifted her arm and waved at her. Brooke was glad the older woman was recovering so well, but there was a lingering worry that ate at her as she realized there really wouldn't be any reason for Jared to hang around much longer.

Her cousin Georgia made her way over and sat down beside Brooke, looking like she had lost her best friend. Brooke had noticed that her boyfriend Logan wasn't with her at this gathering, so she suspected they might have broken up. But she didn't want to bring it up and upset Georgia any more. Grams, however, wasn't as good at keeping her thoughts to herself.

"Georgia, I still don't believe that Logan would have intentionally hurt you. I think you need to talk to him." Obviously, Grandma Gertie knew what was going on and she wasn't about to just let Georgia sit here and mope about it.

"Grandma, I'm not really in the mood to talk about it."

Brooke quickly came to her cousin's rescue, knowing right away how awful Georgia was feeling. She remembered the feeling too well…

"Look, they're about to announce the winner for the gingerbread house. Although we really don't even need to get up because everyone already knows who will win." Brooke laughed and rolled her eyes dramatically.

Renae jumped in at the chance to change the subject too. "Of course. Robyn will win by a gingerbread landslide while the rest of us just wasted days putting our own together for no apparent reason other than to make hers look even better."

Brooke's sister always won anything like this. She was obsessed with Pinterest and always had new and creative ideas for everything she did. That's why Brooke had just let her decorate inside the office this year because she knew then it would look like something out of a magazine and would be far better than anything she could have done.

And Robyn's gingerbread house entry would be no different. Brooke had made a feeble attempt on her own, while Jared had tried to help. But in the end, the icing didn't stick, one of the walls had a giant crack in it, and she was sure there was more cat hair on the frosting she'd used for snow than there was left on her cats.

So, she wasn't really going to be heartbroken when she didn't win.

Joel sauntered over and sat down, looking back and forth between the women. "So, ladies, why aren't you all up there waiting to see who won?" A grin spread across his face, showing off his one dimple. "You never know, this could be your year."

Grams flipped her hand and stood up, shaking her head. "I don't even know why I still enter this silly contest. I haven't won in years, ever since that *Pinterest* came along."

They all laughed as their grandma walked over to sit with Maude, knowing full well that until Robyn had demonstrated a creative side, it had always been Grandma Gertie who won everything. Now her nose was just slightly out of joint that she wasn't winning anymore.

"How come you're not over there rescuing poor Jared? I see now Mom has pulled him over and is introducing him to Uncle Bob and Aunt April Lynn. If I was the jealous type, I might be offended that she seems more excited to brag about her daughter's new boyfriend than her favorite son."

"Oh really? I'm certain she's still been bragging about Travis quite a bit tonight."

Joel stuck his tongue out at her and leaned back in his chair.

"Jared seems nice, Brooke. I'm really happy for you. But I have to mention something that has kind of been bothering me and I wasn't sure how to tell you." Renae looked across the table at her, nervously moving her eyes to look at Georgia and Joel. Brooke could tell she wasn't sure if she should say anything in front of the others.

"Go ahead, Renae. None of us have any secrets we need to hide. If you have something to say, I want to hear it."

Renae took a deep breath and nodded. "Okay, well it's likely nothing more than me letting my imagination get carried away on me. But the other day I was browsing through some shelves at the bookstore and when I glanced at the bestseller wall, I noticed one in crime fiction by J.D. Webber. Now, I've heard of that name even though I don't read those kind of books..." Renae gave a quick shudder for emphasis before continuing.

But Brooke already knew what she was going to say.

"Yes, Renae, Jared is actually J.D. Webber." He hadn't told her yet or confirmed what she'd heard from Todd, but Brooke had looked it up for herself and knew the truth. She was waiting and hoped Jared would tell her himself.

Joel sat up straighter and looked at her in shock. "So, he *did* tell you then?"

Brooke glanced at her brother, realizing he'd known the truth already. "Well no, actually he didn't. I had to hear it from Todd. But I take it from the sound of your voice that you knew and decided not to tell me?"

He just shrugged, not even looking like he'd done anything wrong. "Not really. Travis and Dusty mentioned it to me and asked if I knew. Apparently, they heard it that day Amanda had shown up in their office. But I didn't think it was my place to say anything. I'm sure Jared has his reasons for not saying anything, so it really isn't any of my business."

Brooke's mouth dropped open in surprise. All

their lives, they'd shared everything but for some reason, Joel had decided to keep this from her.

"Brooke, have you found out much about who J.D. Webber is? I mean, I really, *really* don't like having to bring this up. But I was snooping around online after I discovered who he was, and it turns out he has a bit of a reputation as a *love'em and leave'em* kind of guy. There are a few women who have left less than flattering remarks about him online. And there are pictures of him out with these women..." Renae chewed on her lip nervously as she told Brooke everything she'd found out.

"Like I said, it doesn't necessarily mean anything. We can't always trust what's on the Internet. But I just wanted to make sure you knew everything before things went too far with you guys. I don't want to see you get hurt again."

Georgia put her hand on Brooke's. "Be careful, Brooke. Sometimes the person you believe them to be turns out to be nowhere near who they really are."

Joel shook his head, like he wasn't willing to believe what they were saying. "Well, I've gotten to know Jared a lot over the past couple of weeks, especially watching him move heaven and earth to get that ridiculous tree set up for you, and I believe he can be trusted. And I don't say something like that lightly, and you know it Brooke. I told you repeatedly how much I didn't trust Todd. If I even thought for a second Jared wasn't someone I could trust, I'd be over there right now knocking him to the ground." Joel leaned forward and looked her in the eye. "It's up to you, Brooke. But remember that you can't always be holding on to the mistrust that Todd left you with. Talk to Jared and find out the truth, but don't just throw everything away because you think he's keeping something from you. That isn't fair to him."

Brooke turned her head and watched as Jared finally freed himself from the family talking to him and made his way over. His face lit up with a smile when he saw her, and he started to walk as fast as he could. Her pulse picked up again and she realized that Joel was right. She needed to talk to Jared and give him a chance to explain. But not tonight.

Tonight, she just wanted to enjoy being with her family, celebrating Christmas, beside the man she knew beyond a doubt she was falling in love with.

CHAPTER SIXTEEN

"I'm not really sure what her favorite scent would be. I just know she always has candles going and what woman doesn't like nice smelling soaps?" Jared picked another one of the handmade soaps up and sniffed it. "I like this one. But I'm a man and maybe what I like, and she would like are two different things."

The woman behind the counter, who'd introduced herself as Lindy, just laughed softly and took the soap from his hand. "This one is a favorite of a lot of women. It's got lavender, honey, and lemon, so I'm almost certain anyone would love this scent."

Jared sighed and looked around the shop. He'd come into Scentiments to try picking out some little gifts to put together for Brooke. But he knew he was floundering around like a fish out of water and probably was making a complete fool of himself.

Thankfully, Lindy must have sensed his frustration, so she grabbed another soap off the shelf and handed it to him. "This is another popular one. It has Himalayan salt in it with grapefruit scent."

He sniffed it and shrugged. It really didn't smell any different than the hundred other ones he'd inhaled in the past half hour.

"Would you like me to just put a basket together with soaps, candles, oils, and other little goodies Brooke might like? She's come in quite a few times to buy different things, so I have an idea of what she would be happy to get."

Jared resisted the urge to lift the woman into his arms and spin her around the room in gratitude. "Yes! I know how busy you are with Christmas in just a couple of days, but I'd appreciate anything you could put together for me. I'm in no hurry, so I can just wait here for you to finish."

As she turned to pick items off the shelves for him, he walked over and lifted a bottle of oil to his nose, cringing at the overpowering smell. *Geranium.* He really hoped Lindy didn't put anything with that stinky smell into the basket. Just as he was about to turn and mention it to her, the bell above the door jingled, announcing another customer. He absently lifted his head to look, and immediately wished he hadn't. His eyes locked on Amanda's and this shop wasn't big enough for him to hide anywhere. She headed in his direction, a smile that he could only call evil plastered on her face.

"Well, it's not often you see a man frequenting a place like this. I assume you're here picking something up for Brooke?"

He casually leaned against a shelf on the wall and nodded, not really wanting to encourage conversation with this woman. "You assume correctly."

She sighed and tilted her head dramatically. He was sure most men would be finding it difficult to speak around her when she pulled her face into the subtle pout she was giving him now. But he could see through it and in his eyes, she wasn't in the least bit beautiful. Not like Brooke.

"Listen, Jared, I'm sorry if we got off on the wrong foot. I really don't want any bad feelings between us. The truth is, I still care about Brooke. She was my best friend for a long time and I just want to see her happy. I know she will likely never be able to forgive me, but I just want to be the bigger person and say that I have no hard feelings toward Brooke at all." She leaned in closer to him and placed her hand on his arm, the smell of her perfume overpowering the calmer scents around them.

Jared almost dropped the round bath thing he had just picked up to sniff. His mouth opened but it took him a few seconds before he was even able to form any words. "You have no hard feelings toward Brooke? Well, that's mighty decent of you, Amanda, considering you're the one who acted like a complete tramp and cheated with your best friend's fiancé. People like you make me sick, you know that? You never think you've done anything wrong and that everyone else just isn't seeing things your way. All I can say is how glad I am that Brooke didn't marry that loser and that her best friend showed her true colors."

She had him pinned in the back corner and other than pushing her out of the way like he wanted to do, he wasn't even sure how to get away from her.

"You think just because you're some famous author you can come into town and start insulting people like me? You're no better than me, or Todd for that matter. You lied to her too. Have you ever told her who you really are?"

He clenched his jaw so tight he was sure his teeth would break. "I've never lied to her. I told her from day one who I was. If she didn't realize who that meant, that's not my fault." But even as he said the words, he had to push the feelings of guilt aside that tried to remind him he hadn't made any real effort to make sure she knew who he was. He'd been meaning to talk to her about it after his last confrontation with Amanda, but with the big Christmas tree gift and then the Quinn family party he just hadn't had a chance.

"Well, at least she knows now anyway."

His eyebrows pulled together in confusion as he finally freed his arm from her grasp. "What are you talking about?"

"Didn't she tell you that Todd stopped by her clinic the other day? Oops! Oh dear, I hope I haven't said anything out of order. But I do know that he told her who you were. I'm surprised she didn't ask you about it or mention Todd's visit for that matter."

Thankfully, Lindy came over then and shot a dirty look in Amanda's direction. "Everything is ready for you, Jared. I picked all the kinds I knew Brooke would love."

Jared took the basket and pushed past Amanda, not caring anymore if he did knock her to the ground by accident. He had to get away from her. "Thanks, Lindy." They walked to the counter so he could pay, leaving Amanda standing with a smug look on her face.

"Don't let her get under your skin. I don't really know her, but I do know about her. She's been in a couple of times the past few weeks and honestly, I'd rather not have the business than to have to serve people like her. She makes my skin crawl."

Jared punched his PIN number into the machine, quickly glancing back at Amanda who was browsing the shelves as though she didn't have a care in the world. "Yes, she's definitely the type of woman you don't want to turn your back on." He was being polite and not saying the words he wanted to use to describe Amanda. "How Brooke could ever have been best friends with her, I'll never understand."

Lindy looked up from stapling his receipt together with wide eyes. "Brooke was friends with her?" She shuddered. "I can't even imagine how that happened. Sometimes I think Brooke is just too kind-hearted and isn't willing to see the bad in people. I guess being a doctor, she has to have an extra layer of compassion in her that most of us wouldn't." She smiled and handed him the receipt.

"Thanks, Lindy. I appreciate your help."

As he left the shop, he looked one more time at Amanda who gave him an innocent smile and wave.

He thought about Lindy's words, and how Brooke was too kindhearted. She was right about that, but all he could think about at the moment was how he hoped she could be forgiving too.

Because if she thought he was lying to her, he couldn't stand to think he'd hurt her.

CHAPTER SEVENTEEN

"I really am sorry, Brooke. It likely wasn't anything at all, but I thought I should tell you." Her youngest sister, Vicki, sat across from her on the chair that faced her couch. "And honestly, I spent a lot of time with Jared while we worked on getting that tree set up, so I have a hard time believing he'd do anything like this, but with Amanda, you just never know."

Brooke pulled Casanova up closer to her chest, squeezing the poor cat so hard he scrambled to be released. "Are you even sure it was him?" She hated how weak her voice sounded.

Vicki nodded slowly. "It was him. I was just walking past Scentiments and I always look in the window to see what new displays they've put out.

He was in the corner, and Amanda very clearly had her hand on his arm. It looked to me like he was picking things out with her and was even sniffing a bath bomb. But I'm sure there's a good explanation for it. I just can't believe he'd do this."

Brooke's stomach churned, and her chest was heavy as she put her head into her hands. "Oh, I'm sure there's a good explanation. There always is. I just thought Jared was different. I didn't think he would be like the others." Lifting her head, she wiped at a tear. "But, Renae found out that Jared, or *J.D. Webber*, which he's still never told me about, is quite the ladies' man. I went online myself to see what I could find, and there are at least half a dozen women who claim he led them on and dumped them as soon as they started to have feelings for him."

Vicki groaned and gently petted Winston who was purring in her lap. "Do you believe them?"

Brooke just shook her head and leaned back into the couch, grabbing her blanket and pulling it up tight around herself. Kiki was immediately there and kneading at the material to make it more comfy to lie down. "I don't know what to believe anymore. If he had nothing to hide, and if he was feeling the same as I am, wouldn't he have told me who he was? Does he not trust me? And Amanda, of all people. I feel like

I'm going to be sick." She tugged at the blanket to cover her face. When the buzzer sounded to let them know someone was at the door out back, she quickly peeked out with her eyes wide at Vicki.

Vicki stood up, pushing Winston to the ground, who meowed angrily before jumping back up to take her spot on the chair. "Who is it?"

"Vicki? It's Jared."

Vicki's eyes widened as she waited for Brooke to tell her what to do. Brooke just shook her head. "Tell him I'm not feeling well. I'll call him tomorrow."

"Brooke, you have to talk to him. And besides, tomorrow is Christmas Eve. Is that really a conversation you want to be having on Christmas?" They were both whispering loudly, as though Jared would be able to hear them from downstairs.

"I don't care. I'm not ready to see him. Just tell him I'm sick."

Vicki rolled her eyes in frustration as she pressed the button to speak into the intercom. "Jared, Brooke is pretty sick right now. I think it's menstrual cramps."

Brooke dropped her mouth open wide in shock. "Vicki!"

Vicki gave her an innocent smile and shrugged. "You said to tell him you were sick."

"Well, you didn't have to add what ailment you believe I am suffering from."

They were still whispering loudly and if Jared had been standing outside the door upstairs, he'd have been able to hear them perfectly.

His voice crackled through the speaker. "Oh. Well, I could just come up and sit with her then, at least to keep her company."

Vicki raised her eyebrows at her.

Brooke shook her head emphatically. She could tell her sister was getting annoyed at having to be the one to brush him off like this, but right now, Brooke didn't care. She wanted to be childish and angry and feel sorry for herself. Having Jared here would make that impossible.

"No, I don't think that's a good idea. She's pretty bloated and really cranky too. Trust me, you do *not* want to be around her right now." Vicki was grinning as she spoke into the intercom.

She was going to kill her sister once Jared left.

"Um, okay. Just tell her I'll try calling her later." Brooke could hear the confusion in Jared's voice. He knew she wasn't the type to be knocked out because of menstrual cramps, even if she was bloated and cranky. He likely knew something else was up, but right now she couldn't be worried about his feelings.

Tonight, she was going to curl up on her couch with her cats and pretend there was no such thing as men in this world.

BROOKE, I'm going to keep calling and texting until you talk to me, so you may as well just answer.

He hit send and waited, knowing full well he wouldn't see the read notification come up. Brooke wasn't responding to any of his texts or calls and wasn't even opening them to read them. He'd sat by her apartment waiting for her, knowing she had to come and go at some point but he realized too late she must have snuck out the front.

It was Christmas Eve and everything around town was starting to close up. The businesses and houses had their lights on already in the darkening sky as everyone headed home for their Christmas celebrations. He had planned to spend the evening with Brooke, but now for whatever reason, she wasn't talking to him.

Well, he had a pretty good idea what had upset her, but he never would have imagined she'd be this upset about it. So, he hadn't mentioned he was a bit more of a well-known author than he'd let on. He really didn't think that was any reason to just throw what they had between them away.

He worried that something else was wrong and try as he might, he couldn't think what it would be. For the first time in his life, he'd found someone he knew he loved and would spend the rest of his life with, if she'd let him. Maybe he hadn't handled things the way he should have. But he really wasn't sure how to show someone he loved them. He'd never had it happen before.

He looked down at his phone, seeing it light up with a message.

I don't want to talk right now. Just leave me alone. We can talk after Christmas.

His chest squeezed in agony at her words. What had he done? He couldn't imagine not being able to see her or talk to her over Christmas.

But he also knew that if he went over to her parents' house, she had two brothers who would probably make him pay dearly for whatever transgression they believed he'd done to their sister. He needed to wait until they could be alone, and if that meant after Christmas, then he'd give her that time.

Slowly, he backed his Jeep out of the parking space behind her apartment, looking up briefly and smiling when he noticed her tree had turned on. He realized he'd already fallen in love with her that day, and how he wished now he'd just told her everything—including how he felt about her. Although he wasn't even sure if that would have been enough.

He wasn't ready to go home to Maude's questions, so he just drove around Quinn Valley, enjoying the snow as it fell in large, fluffy flakes and landed on the lights of the buildings. It was a beautiful town, and he'd hoped to perhaps spend his life here. But now he wasn't even sure if there'd be anything left for him to stay for.

CHAPTER EIGHTEEN

The lights from her parents' tree reflected in the glass of the window as she looked out at the empty street. Snow was still slowly drifting down, covering the ground in a blanket of white. It wouldn't be disturbed until the kids ran outside tomorrow to try out their new sleds, and families hopped into their cars to drive to their Christmas Day festivities. Her family's voices and laughter spilled down the hallway from the kitchen where they were making food ready for tomorrow. It was the perfect Christmas Eve, the kind she had always loved.

But tonight, instead of taking part in the fun like she normally did, all she could do was sit and think about Jared. They'd planned to walk to the

Christmas tree at the senior's home and then come to her parents' to take part in the Christmas Eve fun. It was the first Christmas he told her he'd ever looked forward to celebrating.

Now, she didn't even know where he was. Likely back at Maude's listening to her grumble about how after all those decorations Jared had put up for her, she still hadn't won any prizes for the town-wide judging. Brooke smiled as she remembered how miffed Maude had been that she'd gone and broken her hip for nothing, as she'd said. But Jared wasn't too upset, considering the Mountain View Medical Center had been the best decorated business on Main Street. So he had been immensely proud of himself that he'd won for the effort he'd put in for her clinic.

He'd admitted he might have been tempted to try just a bit harder to make Brooke's the best because he could pull out his mistletoe while working and be rewarded right away.

Brooke's heart ached as she thought about him. Her phone lit up and she looked down, knowing it would be him. She wasn't sure how much longer she could ignore him.

But she was surprised to see it was a phone call from her cousin Dusty instead. When she answered, he didn't even say hello. "So, I just saw Jared getting a hot chocolate at Fresh Brew. He says he's not spending Christmas with you. Not sure what's going on, but he looks miserable."

Why couldn't everyone just leave her alone? Why did her family have to care so much? "That's true, Dusty. Not sure what it has to do with you, though." She knew she was being snippy, and on Christmas Eve too, but she didn't care. She was tired of everyone butting their noses in where they didn't belong.

"Well, I talked to Renae the other day and she told me what she'd told you about Jared. If that's what's upsetting you, then I don't think you're being fair."

She tried to speak but he cut her off. "No, listen to me. Do you think I don't know what people say about *me* around town? I know I'm not ready to settle down yet, and I've been known to flirt with a pretty girl."

Brooke rolled her eyes at his understatement.

"But that doesn't mean if I ever found the right woman, all of that wouldn't change. And everyone who knows you and Jared has seen how he looks at you, Brooke. You're a fool if you can't see it for yourself."

She chewed on the inside of her cheek as she listened. Of course Dusty would side with Jared. "It's not just that, Dusty. It's everything else too. And Vicki saw him with Amanda. I'm not going to let anyone hurt me like that again."

Dusty just laughed on the other end of the phone. "OK, well you believe whatever you want. You know I'll always have your back. But I think you're making a mistake. I don't believe for a minute Jared would ever be interested in Amanda, and I'm pretty sure if you think back to the man you've gotten to know over the past few weeks, you'd see that too. It's just easier for you to believe he's like all the others. Or, in your case, like Todd."

She sat quietly for a second, unsure of what to say. He was right. But she wasn't about to let him know that. Wishing him a Merry Christmas, they said their goodbyes and she focused her eyes on one of the brightest lights in the tree beside her.

Joel came and sat beside her, plunking himself down so hard she almost fell off the end of the couch. He stuffed one of their mom's cherry tarts into his mouth and turned to look at her.

She glared at him, knowing he was only coming over to bug her about something.

"Was that Dusty?"

She squinted her eyes in suspicion. "Yes. How did you know that?"

"He texted me first. I told him to call you because it wasn't any of my business."

She nodded her head in agreement. "You were right. It isn't any of your business."

Joel leaned back and patted the couch beside him for Stanley, who jumped up and plopped down on his lap instead. She tried not to laugh at how ridiculous it looked when the giant dog insisted on being a lap dog. "Well, that's what I thought too. But when you insist on moping around and ruining Christmas for everyone, then it becomes my business too."

"I'm not moping. For crying out loud, we only got here half an hour ago. You can hardly say I've been moping."

She *had* been moping, but she wasn't going to agree with her brother.

"Listen, I've said it before and I'm saying it one last time. Jared loves you. And if you're willing to throw that away over something as stupid as some miscommunications and accusations on the Internet, without even giving the poor guy a chance to explain, then I hope you're ready to spend the rest of your life with just your cats for company. Because no one will ever be good enough in your eyes and will never care as much about you as that guy does." He stood up, leaving poor Stanley to watch him forlornly as he walked away. Finally, the big dog turned and came over to her lap, obviously figuring that if his dad wasn't coming back, then her lap would have to do.

She scratched the big dog behind his ears and leaned down to kiss his head. "What do you think, Stanley? Am I making a giant mistake by not talking to Jared about this?" She already knew the answer, but somehow taking advice from the big dark eyes staring at her so full of love was just easier than admitting her brother or her cousin might be right about something.

CHAPTER NINETEEN

Brooke pulled her scarf up tighter around her neck to keep the chill out. Her eyes took in all the lights on the tree, warming her heart as she thought about how Jared had brought this here for her. It had to have cost him a fortune to have a massive tree brought in, lifted into place and secured properly, then all the lights and decorations. It had all been from him.

When she'd gone to Maude's, she'd told Brooke that Jared had gone for a walk earlier. She'd then said that she hoped they could work things out because she'd never seen her nephew so down.

Brooke felt terrible knowing she'd caused him to feel like that, especially since she'd never even given him any chance to talk to her about it. She knew she hadn't been fair, and now she hoped he could forgive her for acting the way she did.

After driving around town for a while hoping to spot him, she finally realized exactly where she needed to look. And now, as she walked toward the bench in front of the tree and saw Jared sitting with his back to her, she realized just how much she loved this man. How could she ever have thought she could let him just walk out of her life?

The crunching of the snow under her boots was loud in the stillness of the night. Jared turned around, making her footsteps falter. What was she going to say to him? He looked back toward the tree, waiting for her to get to the bench. She knew he was hurt, and she didn't blame him for not rushing to her with open arms.

"Mind if I join you?" She cringed, rolling her eyes at herself for asking such a silly question. Then she remembered that was the question he'd asked her at the taco truck when they'd met. This time, it was her who had made mistakes that needed to be fixed.

He nodded and motioned with his hand for her to sit down. His empty hot chocolate cup sat on the bench beside him, showing her he'd been sitting here already for a while.

"Jared, I'm sorry for how I've acted. And I don't

blame you for not wanting to talk to me. But I hope you'll just let me explain my side of things."

When he turned to look at her, she struggled to breathe. The pain in his eyes was real and she knew it was her fault. She had to fix this.

"When you didn't bother to tell me who you really were, I guess it started to chip away at my confidence and trust, but I know now it wasn't fair to you. I should have told you how I was feeling as soon as I found out."

"Brooke, I never lied to you about who I was. I told you my name and what I did for a living. When you didn't say anything, I just assumed maybe you hadn't heard of me. What did you want me to say? *I'm actually J.D. Webber. I'm a pretty famous author, so you should know who I am.*" He shook his head and leaned forward to rest his elbows on his knees. He looked down at his hands and swallowed. "Maybe I could have found a way to let you know, but honestly I just hoped it wouldn't be a big deal. It shouldn't be a big deal. I'm still Jared. And sometimes, that's all I want to be when I meet someone."

"I know. And it doesn't matter. Not really. But I let it eat at my insecurities because I felt like you'd kept a secret from me. Then, when I found out about your track record with women, I guess I just didn't want to be your next score."

He looked at her in shock, his eyes wide. "Are you serious? How could you ever have believed that about me?"

She swallowed. As she spoke the words to him, she realized just how completely unfair she'd been. "I'm sorry. It's just that, after Todd..."

Jared sighed loudly and leaned back against the bench, crossing his arms in front of him. "Todd. It's always about him. Did you ever just think that maybe Todd was a jerk and that not all guys are going to be like that? I'll admit I've dated a few women, but I never hurt them, and I never led them on. They wanted more than I was ready to give." He stopped for a moment and stared ahead at the tree. "They weren't you."

As he said the last three words, her heart stopped. Had he even realized what he'd said?

"The thing you didn't hear about on the Internet is that I had never met anyone I knew I wanted to spend the rest of my life with. I just never felt it was fair to a woman to lead her on longer in the hopes my feelings would change. I always knew that someday, I'd meet the one who would matter and who I would know was different. One I would know I wanted to spend my life with, and that's the one I'd give everything I had to." He finally looked at her, his eyes searching hers as he told her everything in his heart. "I knew that woman was you, right from that first day at the taco truck. I've never lied to you, and I would never hurt you the way Todd did. You've never just been a score."

His voice had lowered, and his hand reached out to cup her face. His thumb wiped at the tears that were trailing down her cheek. "And I would never, *ever*, choose a woman like Amanda over you. I can't believe you'd ever have thought that."

She closed her eyes briefly, not even sure how to admit to him how jealous she'd been. When she opened them back up, he was smiling at her. "Vicki told me what she'd seen that day. Well, actually she kind of ambushed me and demanded an explanation. But once I realized you'd believed her, I will admit I was hurt that you could have thought I'd do that to you."

She swallowed the lump in her throat. "I wasn't fair to you. I've held onto the anger and pain, and all of the insecurities from what happened to me in the past and I let them eat at me until I couldn't even think for myself anymore. But I can't let them control me anymore. I know in my heart what's true and I know you wouldn't have done anything like that to hurt me."

He slowly shook his head. "I love you, Brooke Quinn. I would never let myself, or anyone else, hurt you. You've had my heart from the first time I saw you."

Her chin quivered as she tried to fight the tears. She really didn't want to start ugly crying in the middle of the moment she'd waited her whole life for. She'd found the man who made her heart full.

"I love you too, Jared. And I know I messed up and don't deserve it, but if you'll give me another chance, I promise I won't let my own worries get between us. I don't want to lose you." She hoped he didn't hear the sob that almost tore from her throat on her words.

His thumb still caressed her cheek as he laughed softly, tenderly moving over her cold skin. "Brooke, you could never do anything to lose me."

His head came in closer and his lips met hers. She threw her arms around his neck, desperate to hold on to him and never let go. When they finally pulled apart, he grinned at her while holding up his now crumpled piece of mistletoe to show her.

"I never even got to pull this out all the way. You've broken it."

She just shrugged and leaned in to kiss him again. "You won't be needing that again anyway. You're free to kiss me whenever you want." Her heart soared as he threw it to the ground and wrapped his arms around her, pulling her in tight.

Now that she had Jared, she'd found what true love was. It was sitting in front of a giant Christmas tree, being held by a man who she knew without a doubt would never hurt her.

And who she knew beyond reason, she would be happy to spend the rest of her life with.

EPILOGUE

"Jared, will you please just sit still. I have to get the freezing in the right place or it's going to be a lot more painful for you." Brooke squinted as she made sure the needle was going in the best spot to numb the skin next to the wound. But he pulled back again just before she could break the skin.

"No, that needle is way too big. Why can't you just find a small one? It's going to hit bone if you try putting that in there!"

"That's not how needles work, Jared. Now come on. You're bleeding badly and need stitches. Would you rather have me drive you to the hospital in Riston? Trust me, they won't be as patient with you as I'm trying to be."

When he'd fallen, his arm had caught on the

broken eave at the back of her house, so he was going to need a tetanus shot this time too. Maybe she'd get lucky and he'd pass out during the stitches, so she could quickly give it to him while he was unconscious.

"Well, if Casanova hadn't decided to break out and go looking for a girlfriend, I wouldn't be in this mess. This is exactly why I'd rather have a dog. They never get up to the top of a tree and can't figure out how to get down. Dogs are way too smart for that."

He screamed out in pain as she finally got the needle in.

"Jared, I would have waited for the fire department. You're just lucky you didn't break your neck. What were you thinking?"

Jared had come over and they were enjoying a nice, romantic Valentine's Day supper together. But Casanova had decided to jump out the window she'd opened to get some of the smoke out from her feeble attempt at cooking. Of course, her screen had been broken so Casanova had no trouble getting outside, making his way along the edge of the downstairs roof and into the tree out back. Then, he'd proceeded to howl and cry, unwilling to come down on his own.

"I was thinking that I didn't want you to have to

watch your cat die on Valentine's Day, so I should do something heroic to impress you."

She bit her lip as she concentrated on cleaning the gash on his arm. "When will you believe me when I say you don't have to do anything to impress me anymore? Honestly, when I saw you fall from that tree, I've never been so scared in my life. You're just lucky you landed on the porch below and that there was a good cushion of snow to break your fall, or I'd be needing a lot more needles right now. Besides, I'm beginning to think you might be a bit accident-prone, so I suggest not doing anything that will put yourself in danger." She looked up and smiled innocently at him.

"I'll have you know that until I met you, I'd never once needed stitches."

His face scrunched up in pain as she started to stitch it up.

"Are you able to feel that? Let me know if it's hurting."

"Of course it's hurting. You're repeatedly stabbing me with a sharp object."

She rolled her eyes and waited for him to tell her the truth. "Do you need more freezing?"

"No! Just hurry and get it over with."

Shaking her head, she tried not to laugh at his

discomfort. She'd stitched up young children who were braver than him.

"This wasn't how I'd imagined this night to go. I had big plans, you know. I was going to show you how romantic I could be."

She continued working, determined to get this finished so they could continue their evening together. Casanova had finally jumped out of the tree and was now sleeping comfortably up in her apartment, completely uncaring about the trouble he'd caused.

Finally tying the last knot, she sat back and patted his hand. "You were a very good boy, Jared."

He looked down at his stitches and then back to her. "Well, that wasn't too bad."

"Now, just one more thing and then we can call Ciran and order some tacos. Hopefully he's taking orders tonight, although I'm sure he's off wooing Roxie." They'd decided after trying to eat her burned chicken that they would just go out to eat. Of course, that was before the cat had tried to find love for himself.

Jared nodded. "There is one more thing. And I had such a different idea in my head of how this was going to go, but if I don't do it now, it's going to drive me crazy."

Brooke pushed her stool back, letting Jared step down from the table he'd been lying on while she stitched him back up. She was going to have to figure out now how to get him back down to get his tetanus needle.

But before she could worry about that anymore, Jared got down on his knee in front of her. His face was still pale from the pain he'd had to endure, but he had a smile on his face as he looked up at her.

"Brooke Quinn, this is just about the most unromantic proposal in the history of the world, but I can't wait anymore. I need to know right now before I pass out from lack of blood, if you will make me the happiest man in the world by becoming my wife. I have loved you from the first moment I saw you, and even if I do suspect you get a bit too much enjoyment out of sticking sharp, painful needles into my skin, I promise to love you for the rest of my life."

Brooke stared down in shock at the ring he'd pulled out of his pocket. It was simple and beautiful.

"I...I don't know what to say. I didn't think..." She lifted her eyes to his and the love she saw reflected in them reached out and grabbed her heart. She knew beyond a doubt he was the one she would grow old with.

She held her hand out and let him put the ring

on her finger. "Of course I will, Jared. I love you too." She got down on her knees and wrapped her arms around him. Never in her dreams had she ever imagined a proposal on the floor of her office could be so romantic.

"And I promise to love you for the rest of my life too."

He was grinning as he reached up to caress her cheek.

"Right after we give you your tetanus shot..."

I HOPE YOU ENJOYED READING, BECOMING BROOKE. If you could take a couple minutes and head back to Amazon to leave a review, it would be greatly appreciated :)

*You can get Joel's story - **HAYLEE'S HOMECOMING** - on Amazon.*

ALSO BY KAY P. DAWSON

Go to my Book Listing page under "My Books" on my website for all of my books, and latest releases!

KayPDawson.com

ABOUT THE AUTHOR

USA Today Bestselling Author, Kay P. Dawson writes sweet western romance - the kind that leaves out all of the juicy details and immerses you in a true, heartfelt love story. Growing up pretending she was Laura Ingalls, she's always had a love for the old west and pioneer times. She believes in true love, and finding your happy ever after.

Happily married mom of two girls, Kay has always taught her children to follow their dreams. And, after a breast cancer diagnosis at the age of 39, she realized it was time to take her own advice. She had always wanted to write a book, and she decided that the someday she was waiting for was now.

She writes western historical, contemporary and time travel romance that all transport the reader to a time or place where true love always finds a way.

You can connect with Kay through her website at **KayPDawson.com**

**She also has an active fan group where she

hangs out with her readers...**https://www.facebook.com/groups/kaypdawsonfans/**

Newsletter SignUp: https://www.kaypdawson.com/newsletter

Bookbub Follow: https://www.bookbub.com/authors/kay-p-dawson

kaypdawsonwrites@gmail.com

Copyright © 2018 by Kay P. Dawson

All rights reserved.

No part of this book may be reproduced in any form or by any electronic or mechanical means, including information storage and retrieval systems, without written permission from the author, except for the use of brief quotations in a book review.

This book is a work of fiction. Any similarities to people, living or dead, is purely coincidental.

Cover Design - EDH Graphics

Edited - Meg Amor

www.ingramcontent.com/pod-product-compliance
Lightning Source LLC
LaVergne TN
LVHW090113040925
820231LV00037B/1913